STAR BITCH

by

CHARLES NUETZEL

WRITING AS "DON FRANKLIN"

The Borgo Press
An Imprint of Wildside Press

MMVII

SECOND EDITION

Contents

Introduction

Hollywood has its fascination for all of us. And a quick look at some of my books being released by Wildside Press will underscore my own interest and fascination with the town as it was, as it is, and as it might be.

I have lived in and around the town since I was eight years old, when the folks moved down from San Francisco to Los Angeles. Even before that I was a dedicated movie fan, since my father was able to get us in free of charge at any Fox West Coast Theater. He was part of the business, and in Southern California he became even more involved while working for Pacific Title, which did the special effects and title credits for almost all of the major films being released in the 1940s-1960s.

As a young boy I was influenced by his experiences, and then later ended up working in the Industry for a while before becoming a writer. All of this helped to influence my writing output, and thereby I did a number of books located in the business, including *Hollywood Mysteries*, a fact book on some of the major stars at the beginning of the town's history (also available from Wildside Press).

As I admitted in the introduction to *Sex Queen*, some stories get retold, a common factor in a writer's life. Some are so fascinating to the writer that revisiting such storylines is both enjoyable and pleasant. But, more importantly, in that revisit it is possible to take a new look at things, to see the characters differently, and to write a totally different take, a different story. Every book creates itself on its own terms.

This time I considered the following:

Getting ahead in Hollywood demands good looks, talent, connections, timing, and youth. Missing any of those spells failure. For the established stars, the Youth Game is serious business. There are endless young actors eager to grab the starring roles.

And so I started creating my list of characters:

Young Gloria, who uses her lush body to get parts in films, gets Joe in her sights, and is determined to have him as her agent.

That's just a beginning. Now to complicate matters:

But Joe's main job is to make sure everything runs smoothly for the agency's top client, Karla, who plays men like the casting couchers play young starlets. Her game involves total domination, and she demands that Joe be her special joy-toy. She has already been making trouble at the studio, so he either plays along…or else!

Sounds good.

To make matters worse, Joe is falling in love with Karla's personal assistant: the virginal Carol, young, innocent, and anxious to get her break in show-business.

That just about lines it all up. The now the story follows.

—CHARLES NUETZEL
Thousand Oaks, California
July 2006

Chapter One

Gloria pulled her sweater off, thrilling to the burning fire radiating from the dark eyes of Joe Blake. He sat on the large over-stuffed chair, beer-can in hand, tensely leaning forward, obviously surprised by her sudden move.

The tight bra cut into the flesh of her large breasts, and Gloria knew he was already excited by the sensual sight. It was important to make this play count, if she really wanted to succeed in Hollywood. Film making was a hard business and it took smarts to get ahead. Mr. Joe Blake was a big step in the right direction. With his help she would take the first steps into the casting jungle—and Gloria was smart enough to know exactly what that would involved.

"You *did* want to make love to me, didn't you?" she questioned, reaching around to her back and unclasping the bra strap. She hesitated to give the man time to grasp the blatant offer of her words and actions. He sat there as if paralyzed, eagerly awaiting the exposure of her large breasts.

She had carefully picked the word "love" in order to frame the mood just right: half respectability, innocent, and, off-set by her body and actions, down right erotic.

"That's why you came up here with me, isn't it?" she continued, still holding the bra in place, teasing him with the idea of seeing what it now hid. The show was important. Very important. And she was determined to give him one hell of a hot night.

They had already consumed enough drinks to set the mood. The man was obviously feeling slightly high. But not too much so, she had noticed. He was one hell of a hunk; great looking and powerfully built in a solidly lean way.

A voluptuous thrill shot through Gloria as the man half

stood and gasped in pleasure at what he was seeing. His eagerness was exciting in itself. She liked being looked at by men, being desired; it was almost as thrilling as the full course of love-play, but only *almost!* There was nothing more wonderful than a man's body hammering against hers.

"Down, boy!" she murmured with light humor. "Enjoy!"

She rolled her hips just slightly, teasingly. There wasn't any reason to rush things. It was important to make a deep impression on the man. A lasting one, that would reach beyond a one-night stand with a wannabe starlet. There were all too many women willing to toss themselves at men like this. She didn't plan on being just another easy lay to be circulated from casting couch to casting couch. She expected promises to be made and then kept. The one thing she had working for her was a smart mind, and the right kind of experience and background to make an impression, not only in bed, but elsewhere. Push, promotion and investment was all she needed to make it. And Gloria planned on becoming a big star in the Hollywood scene.

Nonetheless, the thought of sexual intimacy with this man was exciting. She slowly pulled the bra away from her bulging breasts.

The man stood, as if hypnotized, and stepped forward.

"You are a lovely creature!" he breathed a moment later, slipping his arms around her body, crushing her breasts against his chest. His mouth covered hers, his tongue reached out, she grabbed it with her lips, then teeth, drawing it deep within her mouth, thrilling to the maleness of his hips pressing firmly against hers.

How she had waited for this moment, ever since first coming to work for Blake Enterprises a couple of months before. She had taken the job to make connections, to begin her serious career as a working actress. Everybody trying to break into films needed money or a job to survive and an agent to get interviews. Working as a waitress, as she had in the past, was not the best way to support herself, nor was a normal secretary job. Working for a first class agency was a smart move. But it took more than that. She could use the opening of being there every day as a step in the right direction. From that point on it was up to her to connect with the right people. The son the agency's founder was a great start! Joe had caught her attention that first day, though he'd hardly noticed her. There were too many attractive little sex-pots running in and out of the agency to make it possible for Joe Blake to notice one of the new secretaries. He was Big— important—and could have his pick of many starlets' strug-gling their way into show-business; willing to spread goodies before any man who might help them.

It had taken a planned attack to get Joe's attention, and this night was the first time they had gone out together.

One thing Gloria knew about herself: she was a woman of beautiful body and hungry sexual desires. That kind of combination could not be beat! As long as it was put to smart use. Plus she had enough experience with men to know just about every kind of combination of sexual combat; and liked it all! This gave her an edge. She would never be used by a man.

She felt his palm cover one large breast, play with its al-ready hardening nipple, making it tight with hurting desire.

Her own hand reached down, found his thigh and ex-plored until he gasped.

"You wild lady!" he admired, pushing her away. "You're really hot!"

"What's wrong with that?" she laughed, un-zipping her skirt, letting it fall to the floor at her feet.

Now she was standing before him with only small, lacy pink panties on, and it took no imagination to know exactly what lay underneath them. It was a sight created to drive a man beyond his limits of control. And it did. She calculated every move when going out to seduce a man.

"Want to see the rest?" she challenged, hands on hips. Without waiting for his answer—for it was written hotly on those handsome features, she suggested: "Let's go into the bedroom. I like to do things properly."

He teased her breasts with his fingers, then caressed down across her hips.

"Please, Joe," she laughed, starting to move away, "I'm hot enough...in the bedroom. I've wanted you since the first day."

He laughed. "How'd I miss you?"

"All those other girls, that's how." She moved into the large bedroom with its huge King-size bed. Lying on the bed, Gloria looked up at the man as he began to quickly undress, his eyes feasting on her.

He had a great body; so lean, muscular in a deliciously graceful way. She felt a tingle of excitement. A shiver rushed through her. He was already hard a hell, and the sight of him like that was almost too much to take. She really loved men; loved sex; loved possessing a man. She was, also, smart enough to make full use of that hunger in a way that worked to her advantage.

But at this moment she couldn't think of anything but the desire ebbing through every nerve. At such moments, she simply let her instincts take over. She wanted to surround him totally.

The need was already driving Gloria to the edge. Trembling convulsively, she slipped her fingers under the elastic band of her panties and wormed her way out of them.

Joe Blake froze, eyes paralyzed upon her hips. Then, without waiting to completely undress, he came at her, his lips finding the hardened points of her breasts, his hands maddeningly caressing her hips and thighs.

A gasp of pleasure clutched at Gloria as she pulled him against her, thrilling to the teasing kisses which moved greedily from one breast to the other.

She realized immediately that this was going to be terribly good; far better than she might have hoped for. The reasons for bringing Joe up here this evening, the long plotting and planning—which had nothing really to do with sex—all lifted from her mind under the passionate greed of Joe's lips and tongue as they played along her breasts, caressed, teased their large, supple curves and flicked quickly across the now hurting nipples.

Then she felt his hand glide across her stomach, down lower to search over tingling thighs, building the hot need higher and higher, screaming through her nerves until all she could think of was the driving necessity of clawing him to her, feeling the full bloom of him surge into the fiery depths of her body.

Then a gasp almost choked Gloria as she felt him move

and thrilled to the most meaningful touch a man can give a woman. Her body arched up to find him, but he pulled away, laughing at her struggles. Then she frantically grabbed him, forced his body against hers, and went rigid with intense pleasure as he answered her call, uniting with a slow intent that drove her out of reality into a new world of ecstatic pleasure, craving the unrelenting movement of him cutting her nerves into fiery pains of pleasure that built and built until there was nothing left but the explosive final ecstasy to surge over her like a drowning tidal wave attempting to smother all life.

* * * * * * *

Joe Blake lifted away from the voluptuous secretary, finding it hard to remember her name. That body had been all hot woman, but in the final moments lacked identity, as had so many other bodies in the past months since his break-up with Clara Henderson. Since then it had been secretary, starlet, tramp, prostitute, and whore, anything with skirts to drive away the pain of loneliness which had clutched at him since the accident.

He forced himself to stand on shaky legs. His eyes whipped over the half conscious form of the big breasted female who had so hungrily given herself to him.

For a moment he struggled to remember her name, then it slowly came back.

Gloria Davis; a new wiggle-hipped secretary who'd made a direct play at his office the other day:

* * * * * * *

When she leaned over the desk, while handing over some typed papers, the low-cut neckline of the tight white blouse revealing all the cleavage necessary to attract any man's eyes, Joe had found it hard to keep his mind on the immediate business matters which had been so pressing an instant before.

"You're new in the office, aren't you?" he inquired, much too huskily.

11

She winked, leaned a little further over and then straightened up. "I've been around for some weeks, Mr. Blake."

"Not around within seeing distance, I might point out."

"Oh, you've been too busy to notice, I'm afraid."

"Afraid?"

"Well, girls do like to be noticed," she pointed out with a broad smile, her voluptuous lips spreading across even teeth.

He watched as she wiggled herself across the office to the door. As her right hand reached to open it, he'd said: "How about dinner tomorrow night?"

She turned, shrugged so that her breasts moved delightfully under the material, and then said: "Why not? At seven?"

So that's the way it started. Dinner at the Jamaica Bay Inn Steak House was delightful, looking out over the Marina Del Rey harbor; it had set the mood while they sipped cocktails and listened to the piano bar. It was later, when they drove up to her apartment in Hollywood (just off Normandie and Melrose) that Gloria asked him up for a nightcap. "I only have beer and vodka," was her offer when they stepped into the small one bedroom apartment.

Beer had suited him fine, partly because he was already feeling his drinks, partly because it had been a long time since he'd had beer and partly because beer would hardly hinder any sexual activities that might follow.

* * * * * * *

His eyes once more took in the shape of Gloria Davis, hesitating on her swelling breasts with their large pink nipples, relaxed now that her body had been sexual spent out in it union with his.

He wondered vaguely what this blonde dish was actually after. A sex night, no! No, they never wanted just that. Every woman wanted to be a star; young wanna-bees who would do anything to get a break in show-business. Including sleeping with power brokers, men who were able to open doors to small parts in film or on stage. They were all pretty much the

12

same; all eager, desperately cooperative. The smart ones knew when to play and when to hold off; some also knew how to really stand out among the best looking, most desirable, line up of young women. Gloria was something pretty special to look at; and damned good in bed. And unlike many such ladies, hadn't faked her joy of sex. Unless she was more talented than he gave her credit for—she had enjoyed every moment with him. All she needed was acting talent, some good promotion, connections and a lot of luck mixed with perfect timing. Success in show business depended on much more than looks, willingness to do what was necessary, and experience. It took that final blessing: being at the right place at the right time.

He wondered if she had any talent to go with that lush, willing and amazingly responsive body.

She was young and probably would look good on the screen. And, hopefully, if she made it to the top wouldn't be a problem to the studios like many named stars became.

Like his number one problem at the agency, Karla Kane, the agency's big star. Karla had been with them for the last five years, but now was becoming a top problem. Harv Freeman had called him this afternoon, saying that Karla was being difficult, a real pain on the set. The director and producer were going out of their minds, and he had threatened to call the whole production off if she didn't start shaping up. And it was his job to keep her in line.

"Joe," Gloria Davis voice murmured from the bed. "Give me one, too?"

Absently, Joe realized he had picked up a pack of cigarettes. He extended one to the woman, who was sitting up on an elbow. Her sensual lips curled around the cylinder of tobacco in such a way as to be highly suggestive, especially considering where her eyes automatically swept. Then she was once again looking up into his eyes, a lidded, passionate expression burning bright. "I think, Joe, that the fun has just begun."

Her right hand reached out playfully and he forgot all about the business problems as realization of what new heights of sexual pleasure were in the offering. Her intimate, quick caress left nothing to the imagination.

STAR BITCH, BY CHARLES NUETZEL

Chapter Two

Karla Kane, her long red hair flowing down over slender shoulders, looked at the attractive young woman who had come on as her secretary a couple of days before, feeling both "motherly" mixed with a tinge of jealousy.

Oh, to be so young, she thought, envious. The girl had her whole life ahead of her—and she was a stunner.

The two of them were sitting on the patio, eating a morning breakfast of boiled eggs and toast. Karla was dressed in a green silk house-robe which pulled tightly about her slim, though curvy naked body. The other woman, Carol Fenton, dark complexioned, with short black hair, deep brown eyes, was dressed in a tight fitting sweater and form fitting short shirt, very fetching, and youthful.

Karla fought the pang of jealousy. "You're so young. And pretty."

"Not really, Miss Kane," Carol announced while buttering a piece of toast.

"Please get in the habit of calling me Karla, or Darling, anything but *that!"*

"What ever you say...Karla—just that it seems so strange, seeing you in movies all these years and now working for you and—"

"Stop gushing!" Karla snapped, irritated. "I'm not all that much older than you." That she knew to be an outright lie; but one she'd like to believe. If only it were true. "What are you, anyway, nineteen, twenty?"

"Twenty-three."

"You don't look over twenty. Darling, don't let anybody else know that. Save your age...you'll need it, later. If you're really serious about getting into the movies."

"I am, Karla...really. Been studying for several years." She smiled winningly.

How young and innocent she is, Karla Kane thought, fighting back the jealousy. *Her whole career is ahead of her, while mine....Don't want to think about that!*

Once a woman started dipping into middle thirties she was on her way towards a continual struggle to keep getting top parts. And, Karla, much too close to forty than she wanted to admit, was getting at the stage where good parts were difficult to get. Instead of that making her more cooperative, it tended to make her desperately terrified. And that was, she admitted, creating difficulties at the studio. But she couldn't help it. Life could be frightening, at best, and surviving in Hollywood was a battle royal, night and day. Exhausting, and damning. And it was a downhill drive through hell. Soon enough she'd be pushed out by younger woman and finally, if she was lucky enough, given mother roles.

Karla's eyes ran over the youthful figure, the bust line, of the girl in front of her. It had been many years since she had looked at a woman like that. Usually such glances were saved for men; but there was something about Carol Fenton which fascinated her. Maybe because the girl seemed so much the virgin, inexperienced, just out of the protection of babyhood. Probably never experienced anything more exciting than a hot petting session. That was of little importance. What mattered was a sense of charm and radiant "something" which just reached out and grabbed a person. She wanted to help the girl. One instantly desired to help guide her, protect her from the dangers, advise her, become a mentor.

Oh, God, that's the last thing I want! She thought, agonizing over those feelings. *This is the competition in the flesh!*

And yet, the young lady was appealing and likeable. That's part of the reason she had hired her. That, and because a mutual friend had asked her to give Carol a job and some help in her career.

There were many men who would find Carol very desirable. In fact, the young woman had a good chance of making a place for herself in films, if merely given a break.

16

How must it feel to be so young and innocent? How many years had it been for her? Karla wondered, trying to remember back over the years.

When she was fifteen a boy had started searching her breasts and thighs in the back seat of the car. Her own hot body, flamed with reading everything she could get on sex, alive with young eagerness to know what a man felt like, quickly started to respond. When the couple in the front seat lowered themselves out of view, the girl's bra already open to the boy's caresses and kisses, it was impossible to control the hot burn within herself. She reached for the boy, curious to feel his responsive excitement. When her fingers searched for an illusive zipper he was ready to almost tear off her bra. His warm, moist lips clasping on her breast had convinced Karla that they would go all the way, It wasn't the last time they did it together, but it was by far the best. Later, in college, she'd roomed with a girl who liked other girls and learned that women could be pretty damned hot and exciting, too. It served as a good lesson. Sex was simply a part of show-business. And anything might be demanded of a young actress wanting parts. There were more lesbians running around loose, with surprising influence in the studios than might have been expected. The secretary of a powerful producer had been responsible for Karla getting one of her first breaks in the business; but only after jazzing her up.

Karla tore her thoughts away from the past and focused back to the bouncy little secretary who sat opposite her at the patio table.

"If you're really serious, Carol, you're going to have a lot happen to you before you make it, things which your young mind can't imagine. There won't be just the men—you'll have the lez element to contend with."

"Lez?" A flush reddened Carol's cheeks. "What's that?"

"Are you kidding? Sex with women! Don't tell me you don't know about that?" Karla couldn't believe it.

"Oh, that, I don't plan on...well...I don't think it's necessary to...well..."

"Sleep with people?" Karla held back the total surprise in her voice. "You better start changing your ideas, young woman. Those that don't put out, don't get in. Believe me, I know."

The ringing of the telephone on the table cut the conversation short. Carol picked it up and talked for a few moments. "It's the Studio."

"Tell them I'm seeing my representative this morning. They can talk to him, afterwards."

Carol related the message and then hung up. Karla looked at the diamond watch on her right wrist—a gift from the first husband. "Where the hell is that man?"

"He's due at nine-thirty," Carol informed her.

"It's past that, now."

"Maybe your watch is fast," Carol suggested.

"Or maybe Mr. Blake had some delay at the office."

"There is no delay when it comes to Karla Kane. There is no watch being fast...I'll have to talk sharply to him." But, Karla admitted to herself, it was the last thing she wanted to do with Joe Blake. There was something about his broad, young body which heated her. For weeks she had been promising herself to invite him over for cocktails; ever since that party at his old man's place. She'd seen Joe in a bathing suit and attempted to get him alone. He had muscles in places which sent her motor racing. Plus he was the old man's son—a guy to put on the string. A woman in her profession hitting her late thirties had to have some kind of insurance. It was young girls who got the juicy, leading parts; or at last those that could pass as young enough, or had the drawing power at the box office. The right kind of lover had helped her out in the past, and there wasn't any reason to believe some one like Joe Blake wouldn't work out just fine for her immediate future. He'd be running the agency in the future. And that kind of insurance was just smart business.

But, Karla admitted, it was more than that with Joe Blake.

A hot, curling surge of desire wound itself through her body. Maybe this morning, before making arrangements to go to the studio. Maybe this was the time to put on the screws.

She stood, looked down at Carol: "When he comes, take him into the study, see that he has a double martini, then you split—take the morning off, do some shopping. Anything—

18

but make yourself scarce. Okay? Be a darling to me? I'll do you a favor sometime."

Carol flushed again and then nodded.

* * * * * * *

Carol Fenton watched Karla Kane move glidingly across the patio and disappear into her bedroom, which had an exit to the patio. She tried to remind herself that Hal Peterson was right, that this was an opportunity of a life-time, being exposed to a woman of Karla Kane's stature.

"Remember, Carol," Peterson, a tall, fatherly man in his late fifties, had told her, "that you will be exposed to not only the people who surround Miss Kane, but also, and most important, the manner in which a star carries herself. It's about time you learned something about the business which you are so anxious to get into. There's a lot more to it than talent. Actresses are a cheap, easy produce to get and very expensive to promote. You have to have a plus that will make producers take notice. Karla Kane has that plus and exposing it to you is my way of giving you the chance your father asked me to give you. If you want to be an actress, watch her...everything she does. Then find a way to do the same thing, but in your own style."

Carol shivered, looked out across the pool to the tropic fern and trees which landscaped the backyard. It was a hill-side lot and she could look out across the valley to the hills beyond, speckled with other expensive houses.

How helpless she felt! All her life she had wanted to be an actress, but knew now that it took more than mere talent. But how could she let a man do such things to her? Sleep with total strangers just because they might help her career. Yet, Carol realized, that was what her agent Hal Peterson meant; it was what Karla Kane had said in so many words.

The front door bell rang, and Carol stood, moved into the living room and then to the large entranceway. Opening the door, she stepped back to look at the tall dark haired man who moved past her. He stopped, twisted around, and then said: "Where'd you come from?"

His eyes fairly stripped her body naked and she felt a

flush eat at her cheeks, hating herself for it. That expression in his deep blue eyes sent a chilly wave of weak desire rush through her. No wonder Karla Kane wanted to be alone with this man. A woman with her reputation and loose morals would find it impossible to resist the temptations he so obviously offered.

It might even be hard for herself if the right moment presented itself; though of course she couldn't let it happen. He was the kind of man a woman would instantly be attracted to, a man with looks, strength and confidence. The way his eyes moved over her said so much. And he was an important connection; a man who could help any young actress. Plus he probably took advantage of woman young thing that crossed his office—moving them right into bed. Or the local couch. And who could compete with Karla Kane? Yet if one had to sleep with a man, he certainly wasn't an undesirable target.

A shiver teased down her spine.

Carol shrugged off the silly thoughts, tried to tell herself that she was acting like a kid.

"Miss Kane will be with you in a moment. You are Mr. Blake?"

It was an instant before he answered. "Yes."

"She instructed me to take you into the study and offer you a martini."

"Very thoughtful of her," he said in an almost bitter tone. But his eyes had not left hers, and they seemed strangely soft, even distant. "Lead the way, Miss..."

"Fenton. Carol Fenton."

20

Chapter Three

Joe Blake watched as Carol Fenton excused herself, still feeling a sense of dizziness. There was something very striking about the dark-haired woman. The instant he saw her standing there at the entranceway, a swift bolt of desire had whipped through him. Maybe it was the unexpectedness. The woman was so different from Karla. And if the actress wasn't going to answer the door, it certainly would have been some meek, dumpy maid. Actually he had given no thought about that, until the door opened and there she was, young, innocent, bright, and so lovely that it took his breath away. Her attitude was all business, at first, then changed slightly as she looked at him. She became guarded, yet there was an intense, thoughtful look in her eyes. For a long moment neither of them said anything, didn't move, and merely looked at one another. She was sensual in body, with up-thrust breasts that pushed hard against the sweater like twin pointed mountains. Her hips swelled gracefully away from a narrowed waist-line, and she had a nice, swinging movement when she walked. Yet there was something about her dark eyes which seemed innocent. She was like a sexual kitten, mature, yet so young looking. A neat combination to attract a man's interest. This was a combination that he found highly exciting. But it was more than mere sexual attraction.

He was immediately interested, and wondered what it would be like to know her; and he wanted to do that very much. That happened at times when somebody you noticed in a party or office or even on the streets. Instantly you wanted to know more about them. You wished it was possible to get an introduction. You are instantly attracted in more than a mere physical way. Sex always caught a person's attention; but when there was more to it than that, something very special happened, something which reached out beyond the biological level. He felt every nerve wired to a high sense of awareness. An instant dynamic which caused him to want to know her in a very personal way. And, of course, that was impossible at this moment. He had come there on business; handling Karla Kane, nothing more. Playing flirtation games with the woman's secretary/assistant would hardly be smart business.

So he sipped the double martini she had prepared for him before leaving, trying to get his mind focused on the serious matters at hand. No games, expect those that Karla demanded.

Nervously glancing around the wood paneled study, he felt an edge of nervousness. Ever since that afternoon party when he had first met Karla Kane on the blunt level of man and woman, a sense of uneasiness had assailed him at the thought of this temperamental star. She had made it obviously as hell that she was interested in him as a sex-toy. And that's exactly how he felt about her. Nothing beyond carnal sex could take place; no emotional crap to complicated matters. In that, it was certainly an attractive situation. Still, strangely reversed; she held all the power. They might make use of one another's bodies, but she would certainly be dictating the relationship right from the start. And there was little doubt in his mind as to the kind of game Karla liked to play. She had a reputation of being an obsessively demanding woman. Even the fan magazines hinted at her wild private parties. The way she had caressed his shoulder muscle as if fairly shivering with desire had left nothing to the imagination. This was the first time he had been called to her house. And he knew what would be expected of him before the morning was over.

If she lived up to her reputation he would be pushed to the limits. There was room for nothing more in his mind except Ms. Kane.

Footsteps moving across the living room caught his attention.

He turned on the bar stool, faced the entrance. His first glance of Karla Kane was like seeing a goddess gliding from some heavenly haunts—though hardly angelic. She wore tight fitting stretch pants and a loose yellow blouse, knotted under her freely moving breasts, leaving her waist bare. The blouse was unbuttoned so that the cleavage between two large breasts swelled about the cloth, moving with every step she took. There was little makeup on her narrowed face, just a touch of lipstick and eyebrow markings. Her hair, flaming red, fell loosely about her shoulders and, while neatly combed, gave the appearance that she had just climbed out of bed.

"Hello, darling!" she exclaimed moving up to him, throwing her slender arms about his neck and kissing his lips. It was the old Hollywood greeting, but gave the impression of being a little more intimate because they were alone in the large house. "I'm so glad you were able to come. That studio is giving me a lot of trouble. But, let's not talk about that right away." She looked at his drink, smiled just enough so that her dimpled lips seemed to be more inviting. "I think I'll join you. Never too early for a drink."

Joe was tempted to suggest that drinks and work didn't mix, then decided against it. Karla knew what she was doing; and she was the agency's top talent.

"How do you like my place?" she inquired, sitting next to him, reaching for the bottle of Plymouth Gin. Her leg touched his and stayed put.

"Pretty nice, but..."

"But...let's see," she said, pouring straight gin into a glass, "let me finish. If I don't play ball with the studio I might not be living here very long? Is that what you were about to say?" She turned and stared evenly at him.

"Something like that, I guess."

"I'd rather get to know you better before we go into that, Joe." She took a strong swallow of her gin. "The better I know a man the easier it is to do business with him. If we can fully enjoy one another on one level, I'm certain we can work something out on all other levels. If you get my meaning."

She look at him for a long moment, then took another swallow of her drink. "Straight gin," she announced, "Strong and powerful. Never liked vermouth in a martini. Even if it isn't a martini without the vermouth. You know, in England they would say 'gin it,' meaning to put a little gin in the martini vermouth. Later the gin became more and more important to the drink. In America the vermouth has become almost camp...if you know what I mean, darling. I went to Germany last year...boy, you can't get a martini of any kind there! Know what they do? Two to one. That's two vermouths to one gin. Even two gins to one vermouth is just too far out for this little girl. So what'd I do? Ask for a triple gin on the rocks with an olive. Got to like it that way. Here at home, though...I mean at my house, I merely gin it, straight and forget the olive."

This little conversation gambit meant little to Joe Blake, and obviously meant less to Karla Kane. Her eyes were penetrating his with such looks that would burn even the coldest of men. He couldn't keep his attention off the soft firmness of her thigh where it continued to press meaningfully to his.

"Straight Gin, strong, biting, just like I love my men to be!" She laughed at that, making the line sound even more obviously erotic.

He had come here knowing what would happen. Having been with the agency only a little over a year it hadn't been until a couple of months before that his father gave him any real authority, believing it was necessary to learn the ropes first. He'd learned fast, and moved up fast because the Old Man wanted a son to act in his behalf as soon as possible. And this account was serious business.

Sitting so close to Karla, it was impossible to ignore the fact that she was as highly attractive off-screen as on. Even for thirty-five—if that was her true age—she was amazingly well preserved and could have passed for ten years younger, if one didn't look close enough to pick up the tiny little lines which indicated a slow aging that wouldn't complete its damage on a highly beautiful face and neck for at least another five years. He guessed she might be closer to 40. The only obvious sign of age was the slight puffy flesh about her eyes, caused by too much drinking—and probably accented by a long night's sleep.

It was hardly unattractive to consider the idea intimacy;

except for the fact that Karla Kane was a real man-eater. Even then he actually was looking forward to discovering the truth about her.

Still, he had to play the game as if it were all business and let the woman make the demands.

Finishing off his martini, he said: "I really have a busy schedule, Karla, and would like to take care of this problem."

She gave him a quick frown, twisted away, and looked at the bamboo shelves behind the bar. "I don't like to be pushed, Joe." Her voice was harsh.

"I'm not pushing—"

"Yes you are. I'm big business for your agency. You can just calm yourself down. You'll play this game my way." She turned, stared angrily at him. "Do you quite understand what I'm saying?"

There was a long silence as Joe attempted to control the natural annoyance churning inside him. The fact was that he had planned this morning completely for her didn't make it easier being bossed by a woman. His natural instincts were being mangled by her sudden dominating attitude.

"Answer me," she demanded.

The soft lines of her face had hardened and there was something startlingly frightening about the level gaze when inflicted upon him.

This was the deciding moment. He forced down the annoyance and smiled, realizing it was foolish being pushed emotionally. Karla Kane meant nothing to him but business—and, no doubt, some sexual explorations together in bed. It was more important to play it her way than lose control—in the long run he had to win.

"Okay. We'll play it your way."

A broad, satisfied smile touched her pouty lips. Taking a cigarette from a small teak-wood box, Karla put the filter tip in her mouth, waited demandingly as he pulled out a lighter and lit it. After taking a deep drag and blowing it out, almost insultingly in his face, she said: "You I could like, Joe."

She reached out, touched his shoulder, feeling the firm muscles there. "You're strong, healthy and young. I like my men to be powerful. You play me right, love, and you just might be able to smooth things over between me and the studio. Understand?"

Her fingers squeezed his arm, then she patted his neck like a prize bull. "My, oh my, you sure are a hard man. I like 'em hard; real hard. If you get my meaning! Now, I'll tell you what we're going to do. It's a nice warm Southern California morning, and I think it is going to get a lot warmer. We'll both sit here and talk a while over another martini and then maybe go into the pool for a swim. How would you like that?"

"Don't you think we should call the studio?" he suggested carefully.

"Damn the studio! They can shoot around me for a day. We have an iron clad contract. They either finish the film with me or they can't finish it. That's that! They can't afford to just drop a half finished film over one day's being out. You call them, *now,* if you like, and say I'm ill. You might add that if the medication works I'll be back to the studio tomorrow on time, and promise not to give them any more trouble—just so long as I'm well." Then patting him on the cheek once more, she added: "Oh, my you sure is a hard, delicious male beast to tame!" She laughed. "Hope you don't shock easily, luv! That line was right out of one of my films!"

He managed to shrug. But he was already beginning to feel a knotting hard pressing his slacks.

"And, lover, I'll be well just so long as the medication works. Understand?" Her eyes swept over his body like she was looking at some magnificent stallion. "I just love playing hospital, and having the doc do his detailed examination…to see if I'll survive another evening at home!" She laughed brazenly at that. "Another line from a hack movie…well, kinda. I tend to expand on them. Memory is getting…fuzzed at times. And I just have to make the best of it. So I kinda improvise a bit here and there. Hope you're good at the here and there!"

Again she laughed, pleased with herself.

She was not being subtle and making no attempt to play coy. The woman had taken command of the scene, the set was hers, and she was writing the script to fit her own needs.

He was trapped without any way to escape her lovely,

26

lush clutches. This was both intriguing and frightening. What man wouldn't want to climb into bed with Karla; she was a dream, and a fantasy most men across the world wanted to screw all day all night.

He felt the sudden tight irritation of animal desire. It was totally impossible not to react to the idea of taking that luscious body; regardless.

In order to get, at least momentarily, away from Karla, Joe moved from the bar to the small pink phone sitting on the stand next to the over-stuffed yellow chair at the far wall. A part of him wanted to jump her body, dominate the scene; the sane thing was to play it cool and let her take the aggressive stance. Karla was known to like it best that way. It was, obviously, a delicate balancing game. He dialed Freeman Studios.

"Give me Mr. Freeman," he instructed after introducing himself. A moment later the husky, rasping voice of the studio boss sounded.

"Well, Blake, you tell me," Freeman demanded abruptly without even a simple hello.

"She's really ill, Harv."

"Oh, crap. Don't give me that, baby. I don't like having crap shoved down my mouth. Give it to me straight!"

"She's ill, has doctor's medication and will be to work by tomorrow, assuming the medication works, on time, no more trouble. A promise." He was sweating already.

"Crap. You tell that bitch that she'll be on time tomorrow and I mean it. Or she's finished here at the studio. I'll drop the picture. I'd rather pay her off and kill the film than take this kind of shit! Better yet, I'll dump the slut, pay her off and get some other actress to fill in for her. And I'll sue your agency—and you can bet I won't sign up any more of your people for my films. Is that subtle enough for you? Get her in line. Or else. "

"Harv, have a heart. You don't want your star blowing takes because she's ill. This is no kidding."

"Who's the doctor? I'll talk to him."

"Look, we have a contract...and our lawyers will hold you to it. So stop the bullshit. You aren't talking to some slob who can be pushed around—she can go to other studios if you give us any more of this and—"

"Cut it, Joe. I'll take your word for it this time, but I hold you personally responsible. She's at the studio tomorrow at six in the morning—and no more crap. Understand? Or my threats change from words to action. And don't give me that counter-suit shit. I'm not impressed. Get her in line or we're going to start world war seven!"

The phone went dead before Joe could answer. He slowly lowered the receiver. Turning to Karla, he said: "Harv's pushed out of shape."

"You were beautiful, darling," she cried, fairly leaping from the bar stool and rushing toward him. She crushed against him, her soft body pressing to his, arms slipping about his neck.

"You were so manly," she murmured just before her lips touched his, open, moist. "I almost had one listening to you speak!"

"What?" he wasn't quite sure what she was talking about.

"A donut, what else," she laughed. "What do you think. You made me hot just listening to you blabbing back at him. Like…oh, you are really hard!" Her fingers were clutching his arm, shoulder, running along the muscles. "Deliciously hard!"

Then her lips covered his, hungrily.

He felt the probing touch of her tongue attempt to find an opening into his mouth and could not resist its invitation.

She squirmed, her tongue dipped deep into his mouth as if greedy for the taste of him. Suddenly he was embracing her like he hadn't had a woman before for weeks. Yet even as they enjoyed the full measure of the passionate kiss, his mind visualized the graceful form of Carol Fenton, wishing it was her body he was holding, her lips he was kissing, her tongue which was probing, almost choking deep into his mouth.

That was a stunning realization. He didn't even know the woman. Yet her image flashed across his mind, lingering there, then faded under the aggressive pressure of Karla's body.

Then she suddenly stepped away. "We got to get to

28

know one another better, before…getting too involved. Don't you think? I believe we're gonna have one hell of a grand time of it together!"

"Whatever you say."

"I say. Let's start right from the beginning. I'm Karla, you're…what's his name. And before the afternoon is over we'll be best of intimate friends!"

Chapter Four

They were on their third martini and Joe Blake was not caring very much what happened other than finishing that first embrace which had taken place some thirty minutes before. Conversation had been light and about nothing important, as if avoiding the obvious. Then, suddenly, Karla went through a routine which he guessed she must have played out countless times with men, relating something that was generally known in the industry, but with a rather teasing twist to it.

"You know how I got my name?" she asked, suddenly. Before he could make any response she continued with: "I was Jane Templeton and one studio guy suggested Jane Tempting. It almost made the grade. But one of the men claimed it was too 'tempting' and obvious—and he put his hands palm up in front of his chest, indicated a woman's boobs. One man offered 'Terry Tits' to that. That brought on a crude laugh all around. I stood and wiggled a little to let them know I wasn't about to be insulted by such comments. And then another guy said he thought I was erotic enough to take on a more subtle name. That brought the idea of Cane, Candy Cane was the original idea. You know, you suck a candy cane. Real stupid and not subtle at all. I voted for Cindy Kane. Again the guy with the handy boobs did squeezing actions in the air. Crude little bastard. I had a German uncle called Karl and I suggested a female version of that. At first they thought Carla Cane and I suggested something more exotic, spelling it Karla and the booby guy came up with the extra K for Kane—bless his little heart!"

All the time her eyes were flashing bright and her hands made moves under her breasts, suggestively brazen.

31

"I liked that name, thought it was just right. It is easy to sign and I can use the KK as a little joke. Kissy, kissy. Crude, but it works."

She went on to tell a few nasty little studio stories of how some of the men had tried to get her in bed and how she'd picked her lovers very carefully. "I never wanted to get a rep for being a slut. Nothing wrong with some fun between adults, and all that. But a girl doesn't want to be tossed from couch to couch. In the business you have to be selective. But now and then…there have been some guys who were just so tempting, that I wanted to have their candy cane where it'd do me the most good. That's how I play my name off when needed." She laughed at that as if it were a great funny erotic joke, her eyes sweeping over him as if she were literally hungry to devour what she was visually caressing. The woman was making no attempt to be subtle.

"You must think I'm horrid!" she announced, not moving, but looking directly into his eyes. "But, I don't like playing games. We both know what you're here for. And, quite frankly, I'm squirmy all over. Let's strip. I want to see all those hard muscles you have hidden under that horrid clothing!" Karla announced, laughing, standing on the edge of the pool, staring at Joe in a very haughty way, hands on hips, challenging him to not take her up on it.

Now, as if some kind of long game had come to an end in Karla's mind, she was moving into direct action, no longer playing around. Her hands already reached for the knotted material of her blouse, slowly, teasingly she worked it loose.

Joe felt a sense of deep detachment, even while feeling an erotic pleasure at this little act.

"Bet you wanna see what I have hidden under this!" she teased. "Bet I wanna show them off to you, too."

Karla's gaze burned hot across the short distance between them. Her fingers hesitating as the knot came loose, holding the cloth still firm around her breasts, she said: "Aren't you going to join me? Aren't you gonna give me something to look at before I really start…doing the natural with you?"

"Haven't got any swim suit," he foolishly stated.

Karla laughed throatily. "You *are* an innocent," she said.

"Almost as bad as Carol."

Mention of her secretary sent a strange longing through Joe. Something about the woman had hit him hard, that quickly; he couldn't quite understand it; still, there it was. The vision of the woman forced itself across his mind, as if projected on a screen. It didn't make sense. Yet almost unwanted it was there, teasing, tempting. He couldn't help wondering what she must be like in every way. Sometimes a woman could impress herself on a man at first glance. He didn't believe in love at first sight, but could believe in lust at first sight. Yet she had not, in any way, been flirtatious. With Carol he felt something else, far more penetrating. Strange. And to have her pop up while he was in the presence of Karla Kane was almost perverse.

He shook his head, as if to shake away those thoughts.

"What's wrong? Don't you like me?" Karla inquired.

"Hardly," he managed, refocusing his total attention on Karla. This was business; this was pleasure; this was stunningly erotic. She was, without question, one hell of a hot looking check, a lady every man was panting to have. And there she was, offering herself to him! He literally didn't want to think of anything but this woman. And it was important that he let this relationship fan itself fully—keep her happy and the agency would be happy and the studio would be happy. And what was about to follow was certainly promising to make both of them quite happy.

He started pulling off his shirt.

"That's more like it!" Karla cried, slipping out of blouse. "Big muscles Hard, lovely, delicious muscles I'm sure are gonna fill me with so much lovin' pleasure!"

Joe froze at the sight of her large supply of breasts which stood out so youthfully from her chest; it wouldn't be hard to believe she'd had them enlarged. The nipples were cherry pink, wide, their points like little darts temptingly pert and inviting.

As he gaped, Karla peeled down the stretch pants, which quickly revealed there was nothing underneath other than the woman.

A quick stab of erotic pleasure knifed through him. There was something overwhelmingly sexy about a woman not wearing panties; it instantly announced her obvious intent.

"Come on, and get what you're lookin' at!" she laughed, suddenly turning and diving gracefully into the pool.

Aroused beyond his control, Joe had difficulty getting his pants and under clothing off. The effects of the martinis had cut aside all hesitation to take Karla's open offer of fun and games. All the stories he had heard about the woman and her demands, almost sadistic cruelty to lovers, washed away at the thought of exploring her silken body.

He fairly ran to the edge of the pool, awkwardly splashed into the water, not caring about making any flashy dive, all thoughts centered in the chase which Karla was offering.

She was already at the other side of the pool, watching him. As he surfaced she laughingly cried:

"You look ready to cook. And I'm so hungry to feast!"

He swam with mighty strokes in his effort to get to her. All energy now focused on capturing this feminine delight. At this point he could think of nothing more than savagely assaulting her, uniting their bodies any way he could, to surround himself inside her flesh.

When he was almost within reach of her, Karla dipped under the water, disappearing. Grabbing the edge of the pool, Joe twisted around, searching the water for the naked woman.

Then he felt fingers reach at his legs, pulling down.

Taking a gasp of breath, Joe surged under the water to discover a watery form willingly slipping into his arms. This was a new experience and he didn't hesitate to take advantage of it. He wanted to smother his lips into a damp mound of breasts that were now surging against his chest, as her hips greedily joining against his. She found his lips, and suddenly he felt her tongue probe deep as her form wiggled, her legs twined around his. The embrace was too sensational to stand. All he wanted was to get her out of the pool. The excitement was driving a hard pain cruelly through his groin like a twisting knife. He was hurting hard. Then he felt her legs shift, soft watery thighs move like a hungry vice to hold him teasingly between them. Then suddenly they surfaced.

34

"Damn you, let's get out of here!" he cursed, driven to a peak of need by her thighs. Flattery was called for and he said: "You're the hottest lady I've ever known!"

"Really?" she screamed in delight.

"You drive a man crazy with…"

"What, honey, tell me."

"What do you think?"

"Do you get tingles all over? Hot where it does you the most good, down in the baseline pipes? Are you throbbing all over to…?"

"Stop that!" he laughed, lunging towards her.

But she slipped quickly away and swam across the pool.

Weak, gasping for breath, Joe followed, slowly, as her laughter taunted him. He caught up with Karla as she reached the other side, her arms and elbows bracing her back against the edge of the pool. As he came up, he grabbed at her.

Her nipple went hard against his lips and he felt her hips tremble.

"Do it here, now!" she screamed, delighted.

"God, you hot bitch!" he cursed. "How?"

"Just do it, you big hard wonderful stud," she moaned. "Come on, lover, show me your manly art. Make me feel it all in me, all of you!"

Joe, at the challenge felt an overwhelming need to show her just how well he could do it—even under these conditions.

Grabbing the pool's edge, he jerked himself up against the woman's willing body. The feel of her under him was maddening. She teased for a moment, making it impossible to do anything but fumble awkwardly, all the time laughing at his useless attempts.

"Come on, love, show me your manly art," she repeated, as if a line from a long memorized script. Then her fingers found him, pulled his form up against the most desired target any man ever chased. She was like silk, soft and greedy, eager to draw him in deep, without any resistance. Her flesh was so hot and ready that the simply glided together, became one united form.

"You feel good," her voice moaned tensely against his

ear. "Do something...make it good. Turn me to butter!" She laughed at her private little joke. "Make me melt!"

Their bodies suddenly moved wildly against one another frantic to consummate their union in a final swift orgasm.

"Oh, fuck me!" she moaned, nails digging deep into his shoulders.

He felt her hips moving hungrily, setting the rhythm. It was driving him out of his mind. The hot wetness of her slippery body moved faster and faster as the peak of need drove them over the edge of control. She held him like a vice in the last moments, gasping, choking, sobbing, her fingers like cruel claws scraped his back in the last instant and both of them submerged under the water, all but killing the total pleasure of their wild act.

Slowly they surfaced and Karla, still clinging to him, gasped, "Inside...hurry...we gotta do it right."

"Are you kidding?" he gasped back.

"Can't you, love?" she taunted, running her tongue along his neck. "You'd be surprised the lovers I've had and what they could do. And you'd be surprised what my body and lips can make them do...you follow Karla's instructions, love, and I'll teach you some tricks you never heard before! Now, out, man!"

The needling tone of her voice left no room for any further objections. He felt threatened through to the core—as any man would be by such words. If others could do it, he should be able to do the same.

They came out of the pool in each other's arms, at the shallow end. Dripping wet, Karla urged him to the door which led into a large bedroom. Her oval shaped bed was invitingly stripped of all covers, waiting to support their bodies in a game of passion.

"Come, lover," she demanded, taking his hand and urging him onto the bed. She moved down beside him, hands running along his chest, down across his stomach, then lower to explore his legs, hips and finally groped him with trembling fingers.

"You're gotta be so hard, baby, you won't believe it!" she fairly sobbed in joy, as her lips moved down to what her fingers so skillfully embraced

"Now, lover, we'll do it right...and if you are very, very good to little ole' me, I'll get well. Remember, Karla isn't feeling very good, and she needs some excellent medicine. Just like she's holding right now. I have to take it, like a good little girl. Oh, how I got to take my lovely, juicy medicine!" With that, she covered him with hot kisses, taking total control of the situation. "Just lay back, lover," she breathed passionately, her breasts heaving, a moment later, "and enjoy the feast of pleasure little old Karla's lips can give you."

With that she once more leaned down, slipped her lips and tongue along his chest, then across his stomach, teasing, playing an erotic game with her hands across his thighs, up over his hips.

After that wildness overwhelmed him as her lips began to really envelop him, greedily as if unable to get enough. She moaned: "Oh...can't get enough of you!" A giggling sounded from her lips. "I'm gonna have me a real cocktail, luv!"

After that there was nothing but sensations assaulting him, furious waves of pleasure as the woman literally feasted on all of his body, without stopping, as if she had been on a starvation diet now ended. He was her feast and she was determined to devour him completely.

Much later he lay back, exhausted from the last final union of their forms which had followed Karla's first luscious lips of love that soothed such erotic pleasure over him. After that she had been wild to know him again and amazingly her body had worked fantastic power over his. Their union was total, her form squirming on top of his like some insane passionate animal unable to get enough of what he could give.

But now he could not have acted out Karla's stud for all the money in the world. He lay back, her head on his shoulder, breasts against his chest. Karla had fallen into a half sleep, breathing deeply, contented for the moment. For that he was glad.

She had been fantastic, but at the same time savagely demanding.

His mind drifted from her, comparing what had just happened with many of the women he'd known in the past.

There had been enough in college, and then in the service, while serving his time in Germany. There had been a German girl who had done the same thing to him Karla had just done. The German women were different from American girls. They took sex as a part of life, without guilt. At least the ones he had known. There was Helga, who, after dating a couple of weeks, had suggested they go into a hotel for the night. It had been necessary to rent two rooms. Strangely enough, while the women looked at sex as a normal part of life, the laws were such that they restricted couples to take different rooms, if they were not married. He had guessed it was some political lobby by hotel owners to make double money on couples wanting a little fun on the side.

Nonetheless, a German girl could have relations with a man without feeling guilty like so many American girls did. German girls accepted sex as normal, a natural relationship. None of this dating half a dozen men at once. If they liked men, and enjoyed his company, and found him physically attractive, they continued to go out with him, and an affair developed; but it was a love affair. You became their man. Not just a swift date, one night stand. You are important to them; and that was quite amazing.

American motels would go out of business—at least many of them—if sex was not considered the normal business they were selling.

Until he went to Germany, Joe had some unrealistic idea about women: that they should be protected from themselves, that he should put up the stop signs.

Helga was the one who had put him straight about that. When comparing American women with German women, she had interrupted him, said:

"Women aren't that different from men as you think. They have desires. And if you start kissing, start something more intimate, like petting, they hurt inside. It is torture, believe me. It can hurt terribly. I'd hate a man who left me hurting that much—because I won't let a man get that involved with me unless I want to go to bed with him. I won't go to bed with any man that I don't respect and don't think he will respect me. Your American men and women must be very, very frustrated. I don't believe in going to bed with every man I go out with—but if I want them and they want me and we aren't hurting anybody...why not?"

Joe, upon returning to the States, took up a new attitude towards women. If they didn't put up the stop sign, he didn't. Yet there were certain girls who he had played it careful with. People were the same all over the world. You didn't go out and hurt people, just for kicks.

Sadly enough, there were too many women in the States who were willing to ball it up, but felt guilty. Girls like Karla were something he found difficult to understand.

Karla stirred slightly. Then her body moved closer.

"Lover, are you ready for the main event?" she inquired sleepily, reaching down to his stomach, caressing the hard muscles there. "Oh, how I like a strong man! You have muscles you haven't even used with me, yet. Let's do it right. Let's party it up all day. I'm ready to know all there is to know about you, lover. I got you going and you aren't going to stop until I call the show finished." She dug her finger nails deep into his side, then scraped them along his stomach, cruelly.

Sitting up, Karla cupped her breasts with her hands. "Give them your tongue, lover. Then your lips. Then you can kiss me all over. Especially *all* over. I want it with your lips and tongue like a feast...I want you to drink all of my body with your lips, and then you're gonna give it to me very wild and passionate and hard as hell. Violent and cruel and hard as hell. Come on lover. My big, fat, hard male beastie!"

She reached for his head, pulled him up until his lips were level with her breasts, and then she smothered him against them, "Kiss them good. Cruel, firm, and good."

Her nipples went hard under his lips. He felt her hand thrusting him to the other breast, then back and forth. Her demands were total. He either did as she said or...else.

"That's right, luv, just me my sucker!"

Then after some time she leaned back and thrust his head to her breasts again, and after that toward her trembling stomach.

Suddenly Joe knew what all those other men had meant about Karla. A man became her love slave and now he had become her new victim; and there was no escape, because she was a big star and could demand anything she wanted. And her still desirable body needed sex like most people need food. It was very difficult not to become exactly what she demanded.

At the moment it didn't take long before he didn't care much what he was, or what she thought of him. He was already smothered by the passion of her to the point where thought meant nothing, where pure sexual need was everything.

And, strangely enough, since this was the kind of life he had been living for several months with young starlets willing to do anything to get ahead, he felt confused and uncertain.

Was this how many of the women felt when expected to service him?

He wondered. Then forgot all that in the wonder of her demanding needs.

40

Chapter Five

Carol Fenton had gone to the drug store for some lipstick, nail polish and other things at Karla Kane's demand. Since the actress was at the studio, and there was little of importance to take care of during the morning, she had arranged to do a little shopping for herself, and therefore ended up in Hollywood, at Highland.

Her thoughts were far away as she looked at the jewelry counter at a long beaded necklace, thinking how nice it would look on her, but knowing how impossible it would be to buy. Her father might easily have given her the money, if she asked; but that wasn't Carol's way. After leaving college, in her third year, to break into show-business, the only favor she'd asked—or planned on ever asking of her family—was an introduction to the right agent. Allen Fenton, while not in any manner connected with the movie industry, knew a lot of people who made films because of his activities as a Real Estate Broker in San Fernando Valley.

"Well, hello," sounded a rich, mannish voice at her side.

For a moment she was startled, as if slapped. It seemed as if some stranger had been peeping in on her thoughts. A flush worked up her cheeks as she turned to face a tall man. Immediately she recognized him. A thrill laced through her total being and for a moment it felt as if her cheeks would flush vibrant red.

"Oh, you're Mr. Blake, aren't you?" she stated in a far too high and nervous voice.

"And you're Carol Fenton. Quite a surprise meeting you here. 1 thought you were Karla's full-time secretary."

"I am...but there's some things she wanted and she's at the studio and there's nothing of importance to do, so with her blessings I'm sorta taking the morning off." Again her voice was nervous, the words gushing out like a teenager's.

He quickly looked at his wrist watch, then smiled down at her. "It's getting near noon. Could I talk you into lunch?"

Carol felt the flush tease her whole body. How she wanted to know this man. The invitation was startlingly unexpected.

"Well?"

She hesitated, not wanting to give the impression of being too interested. "Well...I don't know."

"Do me a favor." He stood there, face intense with friendly invitation, eyes seeming to strip her naked. That look gave her goose pimples. She'd never met a guy who effected her so powerfully; so quick.

"Why not?" she quickly stated. "I was getting a little hungry."

"Great. Across the street there's a nice quiet little place." He was taking her arm, starting to lead her out of the store. "We can have a cocktail and conversation...then delicious South Sea Fish—you like fish?"

"Love it," she lied, following willingly.

* * * * * * *

Joe Blake looked across the small table at Carol, taking in her fine, delicate features, the strong, but sensual mouth which seemed to be naturally shaped for kissing. The unexpected meeting had shaken him some. He'd thought about Carol a number of times since seeing her at Karla Kane's house. That was several weeks ago. This meeting, today, couldn't have been better if he'd planned it that way. Strangely enough he had almost forgotten her in the rush of activities during the last weeks. Just now and then a lingering memory of her had teased his mind, then been pushed away by other immediately matters at hand. But the site of her in the store had been quite a lovely surprise. Instantly he remembered how attractive she had appeared; how immediately he'd been interested in knowing her better. And now was his chance to make a connection. And he hadn't been about to pass it by.

Up until now the conversation had been so general that he knew little more about Carol than before. Plus he couldn't keep his eyes off her, or numb the growingly intense desire that kept needling up through is body. But it was more than just physical attractive; something about the woman caused him to want to reach out and protect her—as if she needed it. Most women were quite able to protect themselves. In fact, most men needed protection from them. Yet she seemed so feminine, so vulnerable. She sparked a male instinct in him. He simply wanted to be with her; enjoyed her company; enjoyed watching her speak, move, and tilt her head. Those lovely limps seemed to curl attractively around each word. She had a sensual, soft voice.

"Tell me something about yourself," he said, pushing his empty plate away.

"There's really not much to say. I grew up in Tarzana, went to Canoga Park High, then later to Valley State for two years, then to UCLA for one, and now I'm working for Miss Kane. I'm taking dramatic lessons and...well, I guess it's every girl's dream to be in the movies."

He nodded, feeling a silent bitterness that such a nice young girl would be exposed to the filth that the industry offered. She seemed so damned innocent, but you could never tell for sure about women. Yet, Karla had certainly indicated that Carol was young and inexperienced. That made her very interesting.

"Any boy friends?" he inquired, studying her in open appreciation; she was lovely. The last thing he would want to know was that she was involved with some guy.

"None of importance right now, if that's what you mean," she quickly stated, looking directly into his eyes. "But there's hardly much time for a social life when you're trying to be a career girl."

"What's with you women, anyway? I should think that getting married and settling down would be much more appealing. No worries. No struggling against the jungle. Surviving in the business world can be brutalizing! Why shouldn't you want to get married? And avoid all that?"

"Why should I? I'm young and don't want to get so involved with home payments, kids, that kind of responsibility, for at least a couple of years. And, anyway, a girl has just as much right as men do to have a career." There was a slight edge of irritation to her voice, a flash in her dark brown eyes.

"It's harder that way," he pointed out calmly.

"But a challenge." That seemed to end the subject as far as she was concerned. "What about you? I'd think a man in your position would be settled down. You have...I would think, in any case, a good income. Your future must be fairly set and marriage would be a logical move for a man. He gets a built-in maid, a...wife." For a moment it sounded as if she were about to say something like lover.

"I'm loose and fancy free. Too young to get into the marriage trap. Not yet. Not for me. I'm having too much fun this way. And, even if my father does own the agency, there's no favors offered me. I have to work hard and make my points all on my own."

"Oh, I didn't know."

"What?"

"That you worked for your father. I couldn't do that."

"Why?"

"Because...well, I want to do it on my own. I want to prove that I can do it on my own, without help—or at least, not too much help." The small smile which touched her lips was delightful. She pushed back a lock of jet black hair from her wide forehead.

"There's nothing wrong with getting as much help as you can, Carol." The waiter passed by and he asked: "Want another cocktail?"

"One's enough for me in the afternoon."

"Could you bring the check?" he asked the waiter, noticing it was getting late. "Actually I have a full afternoon."

He had to take Gloria Davis to see Larry Bershaw; an appointment he'd give anything to break, now. He would much rather spend the whole day with Carol. But, in fact, it was necessary to get Gloria and Larry together. Bershaw would know how to handle her—the man had connections ideal for a young woman like her, even if he was somewhat of a kook. A religious nut, some said. But a damned good acting teacher and talent handler, and that was the bottom line. If Gloria had talent he'd see she got training and parts in small theater to mold her into a working actress. If not, then she'd offered a fall back position for a woman with her sexual talents. He'd promised to make the necessary introductions so that Larry would take over in developing her future in Hollywood.

The conversation with Carol was stilted while they waited for the waiter to return. After he had paid the check, he said: "You don't know how much fun it's been...this lunch. And so unexpected!"

"I'm the one to give the thanks," she countered. Then as her eyes met his, he felt a sudden warm wave of excitement and emotion. It was like taping into some lovely melody, that simply wrapped itself around him, a blanket of silent sound so intense that he was left slightly light headed. He didn't want this to end—he wanted to spend the rest of the day with her. But, of course, that was impossible.

All during the lunch he had found it hard to keep his eyes away from her. Every nerve in him wanted to draw her into his arms, protectively, fend off all the troubles the world might offer.

God, what insanity! he thought. *She's just another woman. Hot, sensual, desirable.*

Yet Carol was so different from the other girls he met in the business that it was difficult to think of her in the same breath he might think of Gloria Davis or Karla Karma.

It was strange, this almost instant attraction for her as a human being, while at the same time the strong sensual, sexual desire. Usually his interest in a woman was just the opposite; sex and not much on the personal side. Women were, to some extent, merely bodies to be used to satisfy his needs. Much like Karla used him—and all men that crossed her path. It was a power game, to some extent; and a part of the scene.

But Carol was different. So much like the only women he had ever truly cared about.

That thought stunned him.

Suddenly he realized with astonishing shock that there was something about Carol which reminded him of Clara Henderson, the girl he was going to marry and who had been killed in an auto accident only some months before. Neither

of them looked anything alike; yet there was the fresh, innocent quality about each which appealed strongly to him.

With this realization came a quick desire to be away
from Carol; for sudden whiplash emotions tangled through
him with such pain that it was difficult to control an emotional outburst. It came so swiftly that all he could do was sit
there opposite Carol and say nothing.

"What's wrong?" she suddenly asked, alarmed.

Looking up at her again, he said: "Oh...just that I realized you...reminded me...of somebody."

His voice was choked, emotion thick in its tone.

"I'm sorry," she said, as if guessing to some degree what
he was really saying.

Then, not realizing what he was doing, he said:

"It happened only a short time ago. We were going to
get married. She was driving on the freeway, to Los Angeles,
was involved in a big pile-up and...I'd rather not talk about
it."

"You must have...loved her a lot," Carol said awkwardly.

He managed a shrug and then stood. "Better get going."

They walked out together in silence. Once they had
stepped onto the sidewalk, Joe had regained control of the
situation.

"I'd like to see you again, Carol," he told her, as they
stood facing one another, each ready to go their own way.

"Yes, I think I'd like that," she answered softly.

He started to say he'd see her at Karla's, then realized
the dangerous ground they were playing on. If Karla thought
there was anything going on between him and her secretary,
hell would fly.

"You have a phone?" he inquired. "I don't think we
should let—"

"Let Karla know?" Carol laughed, brightly. "It makes
me feel like some kind of conspirator." She opened her small
purse, then after taking a piece of paper out, wrote a phone
number on it. "Any time after seven. I'm off work at six."
Then upon handing it to him, she said: "Well, thanks for the
lunch, Joe. And...well, good-bye."

Turning, she walked down the street toward Highland.

He stood there watching, slightly bewildered. It was happening a little too fast to organize in his mind. What did he really see in Carol? Was it some subconscious equation with Clara Henderson—or was it the woman herself?

He picked up Gloria Davis at the office, having arranged for her to take the rest of the day off at the agency so it was possible to keep his promise to her.

Now, sitting behind the wheel of the large four door Caddy, Joe felt regretful about the whole thing. Yet a promise was a promise. Gloria had put on the screws two nights before by asking him to help her out. The least he could do, after such a wild party, was to introduce her to Larry Bershaw. That would end all responsibility to her.

"How do you like the dress?" Gloria inquired as he started the engine.

He glanced at her. She had worn a blue cocktail gown which cut low at the front so that her large breasts showed off to a great advantage. He had to admit that Gloria had the bone-structure and the flesh surrounding it to make any man interested in bedroom games; and what she did in bed was even better than something from a professional party-girl. Larry Bershaw would be thankful to him for this little introduction. What happened after that was up to him. Oddly enough, Joe realized, he'd be glad to be rid of her.

For a big boned blonde, Gloria had all it took physically to become a star. If she could act, played men right, make the correct contacts, find somebody willing to invest one hell of a long time promoting and pushing her—backed with a big bank roll—who knew what might happen?

That's how Karla Kane had gotten ahead.

Thought of her, and the long, session they had shared that first day in her home, sent a shiver through Joe. It was required duty to keep the woman in line, and certainly not at all undesirable; simply a bit unnerving. It made him realize how the ladies in his life must feel. Men used them to circulate around the casting couches. Just like Gloria would be used today. A dirty business. And Karla had her own couch, demanding and very exciting. Though there was something slightly depressingly, maybe even degenerate, about Karla and her desperate need for a man. Exactly what, he couldn't put his fingers on; for her bedroom manners were without flaw, other than the suggestive sadism her love-making implied. What shook him was the fact that he had been ordered to her house for dinner once a week, with the direct command to stay the night. And tonight was to be his third time handing himself over to her wanton demands. Not, hardly, an undesirable event. Just simply linked to that sense of a casting couch demand to offer up his body on her huge round bed.

"Now, Gloria," he began saying, directing the car along Sunset Boulevard, "Mr. Bershaw is the kind of man who can do you a lot of good. If he's interested, he'll take you under his wing and teach you a lot that must be learned. Open doors! I can't do anything better than that for you. He's a star-maker. He'll give you directions on acting, he'll introduce you to the right men. But...I'll be honest with you, there are a lot of women keeping him company who are looking for the same thing. And they aren't virgins. Nothing you shouldn't be able to compete with—all things considered. The chances of getting the big push will be up to you; you'll be on your own, clawing through dozens of other women who are willing to do anything—and 'anything' means just that!"

"My, Joe, you make it sound so exciting!"

He gave her a double look, surprised, uncertain what she meant by that.

Her laugh mocked him. "Oh, come on, I'm not a virgin, as you well know. And aren't I good at it?"

She reached out and put a hand against his crotch, then glided the fingers away. It was playful, teasing and illustrative. "I'm very good, remember?"

"I remember. All too well!" he literally choked out, surprised by her action. It had created an instant erotic charge. "Do that to a man and you'll be half way into bed."

As he directed the car into a parking lot just at the right side of a huge office building, she laughed. "You know I'm willing to do anything at all to please."

"It can mean more than that." Joe smiled inwardly as he thought about Larry Bershaw. He was almost tempted to warn Gloria about the man's little acting cult—and what it

48

was offering so many producers and directors, unknown to the poor struggling starlets, *and* male actors. The game was offering up an evening of sex; not offering parts in plays, films. In some cases a few successes had made it all seem honest. Larry could do everything he claimed—as anybody might with his connections. But the chances of any one woman or man making it were a million to one. Larry survived on seeing to it that his friends in the business were supplied with enough hopefuls to keep them happy—and some were lucky to get more than a quick tumble in bed. It was a dirty little secret, a dirty business; and the bottom line was: the women were over twenty-one. If they let themselves be used, that was their problem. Everybody looked out for number one!

"You don't know how much this means to me, Joe," she gushed, slipping close to him, kissing his cheek. "Any time you want a little night party, no matter how big I get, just give me a ring."

"I'll do that, that's a promise," he countered absently. He hardly needed a young Gloria to fill his bedroom. There was just so much a guy could enjoy; and Karla was out to drain him at least once a week. Playing doctor to her was exhaustive.

And what was left of those sexual energies he would rather direct towards somebody like Carol—if that worked out. He really wanted to know her better and promised himself they would get together—some how.

Getting out of the car, he waited until Gloria joined him, and started up the steps into the office building.

"Just play the game Mr. Bershaw's way. Don't make any unnecessary moves. Let him write the script. And its some script, I'll promise you. He's had every kind of approach directed at him by every kind of woman. And, Gloria, don't make the mistake of thinking you're the only girl who knows her way around men."

Gloria laughed throatily, squeezed his arm. "Don't you dare tell me you've met women better than me. No woman wants to hear that."

"There's no such a thing as better—it's by degree—and what turns a man on or off. And when it comes to Larry, well, he has a special..."

"I heard all about his...religious teaching...and believe he's tapped into something special," she announced, surprising him. "Maybe I can work something out with him...I'm pretty good at making men like me. And I like some of the spiritual ideas he has."

"I didn't now you realized—"

"I'm not stupid. And I know how to deal with men like him. *Any* man. As you know; I'm good!"

He studied her for a moment. "Well, you're a real surprise. Yes, Larry has this cult-like teaching school, but there's far more to it than anybody could guess. He has all the right connections and can put a person very swiftly on the map and on their way to success in this town."

"I'll play his game. I promise."

"Well, do your best. And remember one thing: either two people click, or they don't. If you're lucky you'll make him click!"

"Click, click!" she laughed confidently.

Chapter Six

Larry Bershaw's large black beard was tickling the young blonde's breasts. He teased her with his tongue, then pulled her down onto the sofa next to him. This was one interview which had been great right from the beginning.

He ran a hand along her thigh, pulled her skirt up high until he could feel the soft white naked flesh above the sheer nylons. The feel of the garter belt excited him as he unclasped the stocking and worked it down over her leg.

"Oh, Mr. Bershaw, that feels delicious," the blonde cooed, caressing his neck in eagerness. "I hope you don't think badly of me, letting...oh, that's good."

"Shut up, girl, let the old man enjoy the prize." He bit her thigh and she jerked away slightly. "Hold still."

He had to get this over with, fast, Larry realized, because Joe Blake was coming over shortly with some young thing wanting a little help in her career. The thought brought a quick smile to his thick lips.

Standing for a moment he looked down at the small young woman now half naked to his gaze. She was pretty, a pixie face, tiny breasts with firm nipples. Her large mouth was attractive in a coarse way. He automatically slotted her as a good show piece that a couple of his friends in the business would like because she gave the impression of being not more than seventeen, but cheap and trampish; though actually she was about twenty-three. With her it would be easy for any guy on the make to play sex games. How easy it had been for him. She'd come for the interview, sat opposite him with legs crossed, very prime.

When he'd suggested that she pull up her skirt, she'd willingly done so. "You have real breasts, or falsies?" he

51

challenged coldly.

"Want to see them?" She quickly stood, opened her blouse, pulled off her bra and let him look. After that it was easy. She'd opened up for the most crude, direct approach possible.

Now he moved down onto the couch, arranged her hips so that they could join with his the moment he was ready for her. She reached up, embraced him with tiny, willing arms. Their lips met, open, tongues teasing one another.

Larry remembered his appointment with Joe Blake and shoved her face away, started touching her nipples, caressing her small breasts. He had to be done quickly with her. A quickie. Sampling the women who passed through his office was part of the joys and rewards of running thing in a professional way. Already he could feel the hotness attack his always hungry body. When her form squirmed slightly under his there was no point in waiting longer and he forced himself down violently against her. A sob of pleasure uttered from the woman's lips and it was difficult' to tell if this was honest reaction to him or a well practiced act; either way it would serve the purpose.

It was fast, direct and without any waiting; a fast taking.

After he felt the final convulsions release through his nerves, Larry Bershaw lifted away from the girl, and then standing said: "You're okay, little one. I'll have my secretary make an appointment for you at our next night-class this Wednesday. I think you'll like the guys and gals in our classes. They are much like you, in their way. All willing to work hard to get ahead. If you prove willing to learn, as you are so willing to please, then you have a promising career ahead of you." He didn't mention the fact that it would probably fall short of her most dear desires of stardom in the movies. There were just so many openings for stars and too many young girls willing to fill them.

"Thank you, Mr. Bershaw," she murmured, starting to rearrange her dress in a most casual and professional manner. "You don't know how much this means to me. I've lived here all my life, but never really believed it would be possible to really make the big time."

"Well you're on your way now with Uncle Bershaw at

your side to direct you into the offices of some of Hollywood's leading producers and directors. I'll be there to help you every way I can. We're on your side. You'll learn all the tricks. Just work hard. Do your best at all time. Remember that great Creative Force in the Universe is in all of us and the Loving Awareness of this great Truth will Guide you through every act you go into. All you have to do is Know and Accept this Basic Truth. All you have to do is give fully of yourself to all who ask. Giving is Blessed and gains its own rewards. Go, child and see my secretary. She'll assign you a class. And be Blessed."

His mind was already forgetting her. The speech, like so many others—countless ones in the past— was a practiced line which went deep into the basic training he gave all his young trainees. It was the truth. Before going into his present line of business he had come to Hollywood to become an actor, then went into one of the many cults which clutch about the landscape of Los Angeles and Southern California. Through contacts he had learned a great basic need in Hollywood. Young struggling people, fighting their way into Show Business needed something stronger than mere religious mouthing as the normal religious organizations offered; they needed a voice which would combine their natural eagerness and talents into a greater force, so that they could believe in themselves and what they were doing—and most of all what they were forced into doing—and become convinced that it was part of the Larger Pattern of the Universe.

He studied acting, got some minor parts in films, did quite a lot of directing and finally—after a long time working as an agent—formed his acting school around the principal that need to act was a highly creative force which took emotional and spiritual control over the person and needed proper directing. He convinced his students that not only was it necessary to learn all they could about the Art, but that they must realize their talents came from a Universal Pool of Creativity and that they had not only the desire and the technical knowledge, but also the ability to tap that Pool of Creativity—which was their Divine right.

It was a Big Con, but worked wonders! And sometimes

he wondered how much he actually believed the underlying concepts he "preached" to his "students!"

He ignored the young girl as she left, whose name he'd forgotten the moment she'd been introduced, and sat in his large swivel chair behind the huge oak desk. He placed his hands together, closed his eyes, murmured a *Prayer of Calmness:*

"Blessed be those who know the Divine,
"Blessed be those who know the quiet within,
"Blessed be those who realize the Divine Power,
"Blessed be those who live Creatively,
"Blessed be the Creative Power of the Universe,
"Blessed be those who use that Power.
"Blessed be all the young who come for my help,
"Blessed be all my children and lead them to Happiness no matter where their lives might ultimately lead them."

He sighed deeply, then his huge hands snapped down flat on the desk as the buzzer rang from the intercom at his right.

He was ready, in the right frame to deal with his next bit of business.

"Mr. Blake is here with a Miss Gloria Davis," his secretary's voice announced.

"Bring them in."

He stood as the door opened. The elderly woman who again announced his two guests gave just the right amount of cold business-like air to off-set his own bulky, bearded form with its hawk nose and piercing black eyes that suggested the Prophet or fanatic. The beard had been a fine artistic touch, for Larry Bershaw had what was nicely referred to as a receding chin. He had packaged himself in such a manner as to improve on his near-religious con-job.

"Well, hello, my son," he greeted, eyes feasting on the tall, big boned blonde who moved—or rather wiggled in a gliding manner—into the office at the young agent's side. He remembered what Joe Blake had said about her; great in bed, willing to do anything. The sight of her large breasts, her rounded, angular hips, narrowed waist, sent a needling tease

54

of desire through him. Even after the quick session with that pixie girl, he felt the first flush of animal desire knifing its way up through his body. He was successful in his business probably because of his own endless need for women. In fact that very need has helped to develop the idea of taking advantage of the endless willing bodies that presented themselves to the casting couchers of the town. The film Industry drew them like flies to honey.

"Hello my dear, I understand that you are interested in learning the tricks of the trade. If you have talent, and can understand the Divine Force which comes from the All-Knowing Universe, and tap the Pool of Creativity with every nerve of your body and mind and emotions, learn to your advantage how the Spiritual Presence of all that created the Universe can be yours for but the asking, I believe you just might have the talent to go places. You certainly have the form, face and figure. I've never seen a woman who screams *Star* as much as you do."

That last, though saved for about fifty percent of the attractive young women who stepped into his office, had never been said with more honesty than at this moment. Once before a young woman had stepped into the office, her name then was Blanch Gordon, but in time had changed to Karla Kane. There was something about this Gloria Davis who reminded him of Karla. The automatic recognition of this sent Larry Bershaw's mind into another level of reasoning. If she was good in bed, and if he could get the right people interested—which shouldn't be hard—and if she had any talent at all—and if she could take directions...he might have a second star on his hands. There had never been anybody like Karla Kane to come into his hands.

Gloria stopped in front of him, her breasts seeming to naturally lean closer as if wanting to make contact with his barrel chest. "Hello, Mr. Bershaw. I've heard so much about you."

The voice was right, on the pitch which sent shivers down his spine.

"Where have you been keeping this divine creature of the Creator's?" Larry Bershaw demanded, surprised that his voice had lost some of its low powerful pitch and strength.

55

"Discovered her at the office," Joe Blake grinned, the expression on his face revealing that he had noticed Larry's quick over-powering interest. "We thought we'd let you handle her coaching. The agency's thinking about signing her—if you believe you can do something with her."

"We'll see, we'll see," Larry announced, rubbing his beard in thought. He could think of half a dozen sharp agents who would cut him in for a half share of the girl. Blake Enterprises was hard-nosed; and if they hadn't signed her up yet it was possible to direct her elsewhere, if necessary.

"Why don't you run along, Joe, and I'll have a private conversation with Miss Davis."

"I don't think that is necessary right now, Mr. Bershaw."

"Larry, Larry to you, my boy. Since when did we get so formal around here?" He immediately regretted having revealed so much immediate interest in the woman. The agent was already beginning to put up his business guard. "My boy, have a chair. Miss Davis...you sit next to him, opposite me. Tell me, what experience have you had in acting so far?"

She sorta wiggled into the large comfortable chair, the blue dress climbing up over her knees.

Joe Blake quickly answered: "Not enough to get her a contract right now. But she's given every indication of having great talent."

The side-long glance Gloria gave Joe Blake indicated the man's words to be blatant lies. Larry stored that away for future consideration.

"Okay. I'll have Miss Hendricks place her in the beginners class and as an observer in the advanced class. If there's any talent showing, she should advance very quickly. I'd say, give me a month with Gloria Davis and I'll know just how far she is able to go in this business. Is that what you want to know?"

Joe Blake nodded. "That's just about it. I'm indebted to you, Larry, for letting us take up your time. I realize what a busy schedule you must have." Blake quickly stood. "Miss Davis, I think it best that we take no more of Mr. Bershaw's time."

Gloria Davis looked bewildered, her eyes moving from Joe's to Larry's. "Anything you say, Mr. Blake. But I

56

thought maybe…"

Larry laughed a little nervously, slightly irritated. "Joe's famous for the fastest interviews in the business, under certain circumstances. I believe I've made a basic mistake…underestimating the young man. A promise, Joe, no tricks. You can do anything you deem necessary tomorrow. I would honestly like to continue the interview with Miss Blake. I do have the next couple of hours open, and since she is still a free agent, so to speak, I see no reason why she shouldn't comply with me."

Joe laughed. "I'm truly sorry. We did have something arranged…though I see no reason why the three of us can't continue the conversation over a couple of cocktails at the Club." Then he shrugged, as if realizing he'd lost the battle, "But under the circumstances, I guess it might he more in Gloria's interest to take advantage of your free afternoon. I leave her in your care, Larry. I believe you'll discover her to be a very eager student. Best of luck, Gloria. I leave you in his hands." Joe moved to the door. "Come back to the office this afternoon when the interview is finished."

Star Bitch, by Charles Nuetzel

Chapter Seven

Karla Kane was staring across at the young man who had been so good for her these last weeks. Joe was fairly experienced in the ways of women, and enjoyed the bedroom scene with a female body; yet there was something elusive about him this evening which disquieted her.

They were sitting in her dining room, candle-lights holding back total darkness. She wore her backless cocktail dress that was almost as revealing in front, cutting down below her breasts to show a nice portion of creamy flesh and the rounded curve of her breasts themselves. It had taken a little over an hour to decide on wearing this dress, one designed by a top fashion designer in Hollywood especially at her orders. Joe had gaped at her when first coming into the house; just like most men had when she wore this dress.

Now the roast beef, oven baked potatoes, and mushroomed buttered peas had been finished off, along with the bottle of Burgundy wine. The maid had left about fifteen minutes ago and they were alone together.

"Would you like an after dinner cocktail?" she offered. There was no room in her voice for other than acceptance.

He merely nodded, took out a silver cigarette case and matching lighter, extended the flat case towards her.

"Looks like that came from Germany," she said.

"It did."

"You were there?"

"During the service."

"Did you find the women different from us American girls?" She took a deep drag of the cigarette after he lighted it.

"Some...at least in their casual acceptance of life."

"Meaning?" Immediately she knew what he was about to say. How many times she'd thought about that.

"They don't make a big deal out of it."

"Oh, how *boring,* " she laughed, leaning back against the chair, staring across at him.

"Hardly."

"Oh?" An unreasoning sense of irritation touched her.

"Well, they don't make a...big scene about it. Here the girls are—"

"Prudes? Like my secretary?" she inquired, flashing him a stiff smile.

"Oh, you mean...what's her name...Miss Fenton?" The quick light in his eyes annoyed her.

"Yes. She's a real *square!* Thinks she can get into the business without putting out." Karla laughed nervously, added: "Did you ever hear of such a thing?"

"It's been done."

"Don't tell *her* that. She'll believe you. And, anyway—I think its about time she learned the facts of life, anyway."

"You make her sound rather interesting, challenging," he mused, snapping his cigarette case open to pull out a cigarette for himself. There was something nervous and self-conscious about the act.

"I wouldn't be that foolish if I were you, Joe," she warned, tensing.

"Oh?" he countered after lighting the cigarette.

"Yes. I mean it, Joe." She spat the words out with sudden emotion. Immediately the emotion was regretted.

"Are you warning me?" he demanded a little thickly, eyes narrowing.

"I'm telling you, Joe," she said sweetly, leaning across the table at him so that her cleavage was even more apparent.

"I don't like to be told, Karla," he snapped back.

"A fiery one, aren't you? Well, I'll let you in on a little information. I like you, Joe. And what I like I take, totally. I'm not the kind of woman who goes for her studs playing the field behind her back with other women she knows about."

"You can't control *anybody—totally,* " his voice warned.

"I can control what I know about." She laughed a little

60

nervously. "Why do we have to get on this kind of conversation? You're here so that we could have another pleasant evening together. Not to argue." Her laughter turned suddenly bright—a little too brilliant. "Our first quarrel. Imagine that, and on our third real date together. If you can call it a date."

He leveled his gaze at her, announced: "Don't make the mistake of underestimating me, Karla. I can't be bought and I won't be controlled. We might as well understand that right now."

Karla felt as if she'd been slapped in the face. The cold tone of his voice sent a lancing roar of fury through her. "How dare you talk to me in that tone?"

His silence was almost as infuriating as the words had been.

"I won't have you talking to me in that way," she continued a moment later, standing, slamming her fists down on the table. Dishes rattled. "I'm Karla Kane, and I don't have to take that from any man. Say you're sorry."

Joe Blake slowly stood, his face looked down, mouth tight against his teeth. For a moment he said nothing, then his voice spoke dangerously soft. "There's nothing to be sorry for."

"You bastard," she screamed. "I'm a star, what are you? Nothing. Nothing at all. And you better learn that from the beginning. I can drop your agency like that. I can go to Europe and make a lot of films. I don't need you, or your agency. So smoke that one for a moment. Then you will say you are sorry and you will do exactly as I tell you. Do you understand?"

His attitude abruptly changed, as she had known it would.

"Karla...there's nothing to get all upset about. I merely meant that—while nobody tells me what to do, what I might do on my own is something else. I like you a lot. Who wouldn't? You're a lovely woman, and when I think about all the men who would give their right arm to be sitting here with you like I am, it really shakes me up. Why would I go and ruin a beautiful friendship? One which has hardly...started, at that? I just don't like to be pushed—you should know better than to shove a man too far."

He laughed nervously and reached out and touched her arm.

Karla shook him away. "You'll touch me when I tell you to. Understand?"

Silence burned between them, then she shrugged. "I'm sorry. It was a hard day at the studio. They were after my hide, making things as difficult as possible. I need a little medicine …and maybe more than just once a week. You're a wonderful doc to my needy bod. You can do a lot of good for me, Joe. I like the way you come on. You come on strong. Let's split this room. I want us to be friendlier. Cozy. Hot and intimate. Okay?"

She leaned close, kissed his cheek. "You smell good, Joe. Real good. Like a strong, sexy man. Now we gotta get you sweating a little...I like the smell of a sweating man, it excites me real good." She laughed and moved out of the room, then hesitated in the hallway. "Let's go to my beach home. It's beautiful there, and all locked away from any public eyes. We can have a lot of fun there and yes, I'd like that." She grabbed his arm, half shoved him toward the front door. "Drive me to the beach. We can stop off for some cocktails and then to the beach house. Then…you can serve me up with your personal cocktail!"

* * * * * * *

His head was swimming from the drinks and now looking up at Karla as she stood over him, the sand at his back, Joe felt a sinking feeling that he'd been through all this before; though never quite like this.

She raised her skirt high above her hips, and then laughed. She was drunk, the wind blowing her long hair wildly.

A moment later she pulled the dress off and threw it on the sand to his right. The half bra revealed her uplifted nipples. She leaned down. "Kiss me, you bastard."

She clawed his head to her breasts and he felt almost sick. Her fingers cut at his shoulder, right through the shirt. A moment later she shoved him back on the sand, stepped back. A quick motion and her bra had been tossed on top of her dress. "Get undressed, Mr. Studman."

"Stop calling me that."

"Stud. Stud. Mr. Stud…man! Man alive you're a real hard stallion stud…man! That's the only thing you men are. Just lover studs that make girls feel dirty and great all over. Get undressed. Karla Kane wants to see you naked again. Nobody can see us from here. We have total privacy. Nothing like a hot cocktail on the beach, says I."

She slipped off her underskirt. "Stud, it is cold. I have goose pimples all over." She laughed as if at a private, vulgar joke. "Well, almost all over, Mr. Stud…man!"

He leaped to his feet, grabbed her shoulders. "I said stop using that damned word."

Her face taunted his, her lips opened and she licked out her tongue. "Kiss the goose flesh away—even where you don't find it...and I'll call you whatever you want to be called, okay?"

Her hands started pulling his shirt from the suit pants, and then she caressed his naked sides with long sharp fingernails. "I'm hot all over, now. You feel great. Let's get you out of the rest of this stuff."

He fought the desire which heatedly threaded itself through him at her touches, which became more and more exciting as she started undressing him. On her knees, she clasped herself around his waist, hugging her lips to his stomach. "Come on down here, love, and let me know it. I want it so bad I can't stand myself." She pulled at him, and like a slave he moved to her call.

The terrible anger which had stripped him after dinner had never once completely burned itself out. And now all he could think about was getting even in some way. He'd heard about Karla and her liking for more violent loving—the kind which she had not demanded yet. Now for the first time in his life he wanted to do something violent and it did not matter that to this bitch it might be pure heaven.

He wanted to beat the hell out of her.

The violence hit him so quickly that before he realized what was happening, Joe moved down against her, his hands grabbing her shoulders, violently squeezing, smashing her back against the sand.

"You'll get it, you bitch."

"Yes," she cried, grinning happily. "I'm a bitch. A real Star Bitch and loved it! Be a savage archer and shoot right into my bull's-eye!"

Her eyes challenged him, and her hand clawed cruelly into his shoulders, urging him to the very edge of violence. That quickly. Something instinctive in the woman knew exactly what to do to dive his passions to a raw peak—and right in the direction she wanted them to go. "Violate me, honey. I want it real bad!"

When he hesitated she snapped: "I like being pushed, luv! You shit stud, do something wild! And now! I mean it! Do me good or I'll tell daddy on you! I'm a bad little girl and need being taught a lesson. You know how it is." She laughed in pleasure. "I love violent lovemaking!"

To illustrate her need, she scraped sharp nails into his flesh, and it felt as if she'd drawn blood. "Come on, love, you aren't afraid to smack me around a little, are you?"

Those nails dug deeper into his flesh. "Do it...or I'll rip the skin right off!"

The pain was real, sharp, and cruel. Her eyes glared at him, silently saying she'd keep clawing until he reacted.

That's when he slapped her face so hard that it must have hurt terribly. It was the first time he'd ever hit a woman, and immediately it sobered him.

Her laughter, the trembling of her body under his was shocking. The sudden lustful expression on Karla's face was almost grotesque.

"Oh, love...love...love," she gulped, overwhelmed with such passion that all Joe could do was look down at her writhing form with total alarm and detached horror.

He was furious at her; and for a moment had forgotten why. The early argument had set things up for this moment of violence. It was almost as if the woman had guessed the truth; but that could hardly be possible.

The anger had all happened because of a woman he hardly knew. Carol Fenton. He had wanted to see Carol and the argument with Karla had started earlier had set things up for this very moment. It didn't matter why; but his reaction to this Star Bitch was overwhelming fury. Yet his body ached to ravish her.

Then Karla was clawing at him, demanding like she hadn't even come close to doing before. Suddenly he realized that up until now she'd been in control, cool, going through practiced motions. Now she was helplessly enveloped in a new dimension of desire, lost in a sea of passion which totally controlled her actions. Being slapped had sent her right down a new, uncontrolled road of wanton need. She had loved it! This washed out across Joe in such a powerful flood that it captured his body, drowning him in its deluge. Her hands, lips, body were screaming all over him at once, kissing caressing, directing, submitting, tangled completely in almost insane actions, clawing, hurting until it was impossible to keep from violently hurting her in return in order to defend himself.

Under the soft glow of the full moon, stars twinkling from the darkened night sky, the murmuring ocean playing out its background music, the two of them fought out their sex game like animals, unrestrained, with total unconcern for the other's natural rhythm. Their two forms moved faster and faster on the naked beach, pounded at one another in the final moments with the hard cadence of the ocean. It was as if the waves were mocking the two human beasts of prey, hissing its continued, raging applause at their passion starved bodies.

When he fell away from Karla Kane all he could do was think about the desire to run and never stop running until countless miles had been placed between the two of them. A sick inner pain knotted at the pit of his stomach as he lay back on the sand, breathing hard, his body and back aching from her brutal attack on it.

"Lover, oh, lover. That's what a woman wants," Karla sobbed, moving to him, throwing her arms about his neck. "A man who knows how to treat her...the way a man should. Dominating. Almost brutally demanding. You savaged me to madness. I loved it. Just loved it. Oh, those muscles. They make me feel all woman...all over."

Then she relaxed against him, and with a last gasp of contentment seemed to fall unconscious.

STAR BITCH, BY CHARLES NUETZEL

Chapter Eight

Gloria marveled at the huge, almost Gothic house in which Larry Bershaw lived and held his private classes in both the Art of acting and the "Art of Spiritual Power and Creative Sources," as he called it.

The moon was high, reflecting through the huge double doors that led to the large balcony just outside. The two of them were sitting at a large, heavy wood dining table, beautifully hand-carved, a lacy tablecloth only half covering it. Silver candlesticks supported slender white candles, already half burned down. They had finished a delightfully prepared five course dinner of rare beef, smothered in its own natural juices, peeled potatoes baked in the oven with the roast, carrots in creamy butter and onion sauce, served with a different wine with each course. Shrimp Cocktail had given them a light white Rhine wine, the meat with a French imported red wine. Now he opened a bottle of champagne as his male servant served a large bowl of salad.

"Oil and vinegar dressing, spiced with the right herbs, only as Charlie here can make it. This, with a light German Sparkling Wine, just before imported cheese and brandy with coffee, makes for a perfect evening when shared with such a delightful young vision as you are, Gloria," he announced, pouring the champagne into her thin stemmed glass.

"Boy, you really know how to live!" she exclaimed, feeling already stuffed and drunk. 'With this kind of meal a girl can't keep her figure."

"Never worry about your figure, lovely one. It will take care of itself, if you but tap into the Divine Power. Eat, work, love, drink, exercise right and you never have to worry about overeating or getting extra pounds." He touched his stomach, which was a little on the heavy side. "But, of course, I never get a chance to exercise enough. *You* will, my dear. You'll get all the exercise you need. I believe in the fine art of fencing to keep the body trimmed. Though, again, I don't get enough chance to practice. Business keeps me pretty active in a chair...and then, I do like a good meal. I insist on a full meal every night, much like this one. That's my trouble. Like food and wine and women." He eyed her low-cut neckline. "You are surely all woman. To you!" The glass in his hand made a dip before reaching his bearded lips.

Gloria puzzled over him as she sipped the champagne. Everything had been totally different than she'd imagined it would be. When Joe Blake left her at Bershaw's office that day, she'd expected him to make a pass right into her panties. Instead he merely talked with her. Some of the conversation had been questions about her past, but for the most part he had merely talked about show-business in a general manner. After some time, he suggested that she come up to his house in the Hollywood hills for dinner that night, then told her to report back to Mr. Blake.

Joe Blake had made out a standard contract for her to sign, which she realized was nothing more than an option to tie her up for six months if she showed promise with Bershaw. But this was enough to set her excitement at a high level.

"Now, dear," Larry Bershaw said, once he had finished his salad. "Let me know something more about yourself."

"I've been around enough to know that the less a man knows the better it is for him." She smiled, then winked.

"You are a wicked one, that's for sure." He took a piece of imported Swiss cheese from a large platter between them. "Very good...you must try it." Then after finishing it off, he said: "Okay, if necessary, a past can be made for you." He eyed her seriously for a moment, then nodded. "There is no doubt about it, Gloria, you have star elements about you. Some women do, some don't."

She laughed, then tossed her head, a little embarrassed under his level gaze; it was impossible to tell what the man was really thinking.

"If I gave you a dollar for every woman you have said

that to, you'd be rich."

He chuckled, deep in his chest. "You're quite right. Though I have little use for much more money than I'm already making." He considered her, then said: "I'll tell you this much, Gloria, that I charge as much as a thousand dollars a month to train the students. I believe we could work out something a little different—don't you?"

"Meaning?" Her voice was even, controlled, though a sudden surge of excitement jarred through her. All day she'd been thinking about what it might be like with the very important Larry Bershaw. She'd known a lot of men in her life—but none quite like this one. He gave the appearance of great strength, like some Lord or God. The beard was exciting and she wondered what it would feel like moving across her body, touching her naked breasts.

"Meaning, my child, anything you want it to mean. But, most of all, you must understand that I am a very *mean* man when it comes to money and I'll do almost anything to get money. But when a real possible talent comes along, I want to make it as easy for them as possible. Now...what would you suggest would be worth what I'm willing to give you for free—in cash?" He leaned across the table, staring at her with those penetrating dark eyes, sending shivers of strange emotion through her whole frame.

"I don't know what you have in mind, Larry, but whatever it is...please continue. I'm not a prude, if that's what's bothering you. Why don't we just lay it on the line?" Her words were bold, but there was an excited tremor to her voice. This was one of those moments she had dreamed about; the time when a free attitude toward men and sex was going to pay off in vivid colors.

"Okay, I'll lay it on the line. I think you could probably make some kind of mark in the movies with the right guidance, and I'm willing to give it to you—but obviously not just for the pleasure of helping a fellow human being—even if it is blessed to give, it is just as blessed to receive. *Twenty percent of what you make for the next five years.*"

The last was stated in such a deadly serious and businesslike manner that it took Gloria's breathe away. It was the last thing she expected. Her mind had fashioned some sexual deal he'd put on the table. It left her both disappointed and startled.

Extending her hand, she said, "That's a deal"

"Now," he breathed, grinning, "Let's stop all this chit-chat and get down to the real business at hand. You are a lovely woman and I believe it would not be too far out of line to make a pass at you."

He stood, reached a hand for hers. Leading her out of the large dining room, he took her up a flight of steps which led to a large upper floor. The house was large enough to room twenty people, and the second floor was devoted to some ten bedrooms. He showed her a couple, which had large double beds, huge bay-windows facing the city of Hollywood far below, which displayed itself as a mass of lights strung in long rows that crisscrossed each other. It was a startlingly clear night for Southern California with little smog to deaden the view.

Finally he came to a room at the end of a long hallway.

"This," he announced, starting to open the door, "is a very interesting room."

He ushered her into a room of mirrors. Every wall, other than the windows, were plastered with shiny, highly polished mirrors from floor to ceiling, angled in such a manner as to give total visibility of all sides of any object in the middle of the room. A large, four poster bed was centered in the middle of the floor, with an even amount of space on all sides. A bedspread of gold covered the bed, and two golden pillows rested at its head.

"How do you like it?" he inquired, closing the door behind him.

"A little unusual," she laughed nervously.

"*Very* unusual, considering the kind of view it offers. The window is just one way, nobody can see in! I don't know if my sexual tastes are strange or perverted or just unusual" He shrugged. "It really doesn't matter, actually, as long as I freely accept what I like and go about getting it with people who don't mind." He pulled off his dinner jacket and then started with his shirt. "My dear, please don't stand on ceremony. Obviously you are a mature, worldly woman, and I don't believe you have anything against the kind of

70

sport this room offers. In fact, I would suspect that you are rather looking forward to the fun I've planned for us."

A shiver moved down Gloria's spine. She'd known a lot of guys, but this one beat it all out. He was casually accepting the fact that she would not only let him, but wanted him to make love to her. No build up, no fancy lines, no passes; just direct acceptance of what they would do.

He waved his arms at the mirrors. "They give a beautiful view of what you are doing. The ceiling, too, if you notice, has mirrors on them." He slipped out of his slacks, then pulled off his under shirt. The mass of hair on his chest was almost solid, black and curly.

A tingle of pleasure lanced through Gloria. Only once before had she been taken by a man with such a hairy chest—it had felt good against her breasts.

"There's a beauty about two people making love. Like some artistic dance. Nothing like it, Gloria. I don't know if you've ever seen another couple during their ultimate pleasure...its nothing like watching yourself as that pleasure moves through nerves and body. I think there is nothing more beautiful or exciting." He sat on the edge of the bed, as she began slipping out of her dress.

Gloria raised her arms high above her head, stretched. Then she released the clasp of her bra,

"You have delightful ones," he murmured, reaching for her. "Come here."

She helplessly slipped toward him, fascinated at the wild animal look in his eyes.

When she stood in front of him, his lips were just level with her breasts. He teased her with a quick kiss on each nipple, which felt delicious.

"They taste good, Gloria; Real soft and good."

Then his beard was smothering them as she squirmed against the voluptuous tongue kisses that immediately worked hot fire through her.

His hands grabbed her thighs, pressing in hard and the pain was strange pleasure. She looked at the reflection of their two forms in the mirror opposite and felt a new wave of pleasure at watching the reflected lovers. The bearded man was deep against the woman's breasts. A tremble rushed

71

over the female form as the man's hands caressed along firm, smooth thighs. Then in the mirror she saw the man stand, already aroused to a harsh peak, as ready for her as she felt ready for him.

Suddenly the man slapped out a hand, digging fingers into her shoulder, throwing her onto the bed. She fell backwards and could hardly catch her breath when the heavy force of his body slapped against hers, ripping at her with brutal power. Then she knew the delicious first moment as he became a very important part of her. The forms which reflected on the ceiling mirror were tensely together, frozen, unmoving as they took in each split moment of the first surge of pleasure at their union. She wanted to squeeze every joy out of this moment, she wanted to hold him tight, captured totally, her complete love slave, to feel all the tingling excitement which he could offer only in this manner.

"Oh, this *is* good!" she cried, watching the expression on her own face. The hot burning tension of animal lust grew and grew as she studied every little detail of her face reacting to the pleasure so totally hers.

A tremor shot through her, and she saw the female reflection writhe under the heavy bulk of the man.

As he lifted away and then slipped down against her so that the curly hairs of his chest tickled her breasts and nipples, Gloria felt a surging wave of greedy need frustrate her.

"Oh, Larry...please...please don't wait any longer. Again...please, oh, please," she moaned, clawing at his back, burning for him to unite with her again and not leave her ever until the ultimate pleasure had burned away the hurt that attacked every nerve, screaming for relief which only a man's body could give.

He chuckled. "Waiting makes it better, big woman."

He kissed her lips, and she greedily pulled his tongue deep into her mouth, hard, all but devouring it in her hunger. The feel of his excitement against her was too much to stand and suddenly she was thrashing on the bed, moving in wild erotic motions in her attempt to capture him.

Suddenly Larry slapped her face so hard that her ears rang. A blurred wave of overwhelming need attacked Gloria and she was suddenly out of her mind, clawing, writhing, not

72

even knowing what she was actually doing.

"Do it. *Do* it!" The voice cried out into the room like the yell of a wounded beast totally insane and without reason.

The heavy form lifted away and suddenly she was very alone. How long she lay there, Gloria didn't know. It seemed an eternity.

She opened her eyes just in time to see the man start to move back to her, his eyes wild like something from a mad house. Terror struck for the first time, but waved away at what he began doing to her. The need, the driving crazed burn of her nerves went wild and all she could do was lay there thrashing on the bed while he started kissing her, his beard teasing, tickling, and scratching. Then suddenly he moved again and his body slid down to join the hot pains that centered through her whole being.

What kind of beast was this? Her mind sobbed even as the dance of passion thrust her body through all the steps of love-play, arching, throbbing against the whole pleasure of him. It was like nothing she had ever experienced, and in the end she remembered to open her eyes, to watch the glory of their ultimate pleasure reflected in the mirrors above them.

That final instant, as the last convulsive explosion locked them tightly in a total embrace, was so powerfully complete that Gloria almost instantly slipped into an unconscious sleep, unable to move or think or dream. Of all the men she had known in the past there had never been one quite like Larry Bershaw. He'd done things to her that were simply wild. Maybe they were unusual, different, and strange to most men, but suddenly Gloria realized that the important thing in her life was having him drive her wild like that once again, and forever.

When the sleep had finally washed away, Gloria abruptly awoke to discover that Larry Bershaw was standing at the foot of the bed, simply looking at her. A strange, almost fanatic expression burned in his brooding eyes.

"You're good, my child. You're very good. I think we are going to get along famously. What do you think?"

She slowly slipped from the bed, feeling wonderful, stretched, watched the reflection of her breasts surge upwards. She admired her figure and knew it was terribly good.

Larry Bershaw grinned. "You are a goddess. You are truly a goddess."

"And," she cooed, stepping close to him, embracing his barrel-chested hairy body to her, "you are like a god."

He laughed again and squeezed her buttocks hard. "Well, my pet. I think you want some more punishment. Is that it?"

She shivered. "You are a bastard for what you did to me."

"You liked it, didn't you?" he inquired, leading her to the bed. "You liked a little rough teasing, didn't you, my child?"

"I think I'd like anything you'd do to me," she announced with a tremor.

"We'll see, my child. We'll see. You've experienced nothing...*I* have a whole workshop of tricks...and if I'm right, you just might fit most of them." He laughed, said: "There isn't a thing I wouldn't do, sexually. I like it all. Every form of pleasure is merely some new form of the art. Sex can take many shapes. While I sometimes like to be cruel to a woman, I think I like a woman to be cruel to me. Think you can tease me like I did you. Think you can make me to out of my mind like I made you go out of your mind?"

He lay back, said: "Tease me a little, child. Tease me any way you like. I don't give one damn what you do, just so its delightful and ends up great."

A laugh choked to quick silent pleasure as Gloria decided on a target and attacked with everything she had.

Chapter Nine

Joe Blake sat in his small private office, thinking about last night and hating it. Not that Karla Kane wasn't a beautiful and desirable woman, but he had never liked to be brutal to anything. Hitting her like he had still sent sparks of shame through him.

His thoughts shifted swiftly to Carol Fenton. He'd been thinking about her all day. Their lunch together had been delightful; just yesterday. Once he'd picked up the phone to dial her number, then remembered she wouldn't be home before seven.

Suddenly he decided to call Karla's place. If Carol answered it would be easy to make a quick date.

He dialed.

A moment later a lilting feminine voice sounded over the receiver.

"Carol, Joe Blake. Quick. Tonight at your place six thirty. I'll take you to dinner. Okay?"

"I'm sorry, sir, you have the wrong number. I understand...Yes—but you better call the operator. Yes. I'm glad to help you. Sorry you had the wrong number." Then she hung up.

Joe looked at the phone, puzzled. He hoped that the yes was agreement to his offer.

The other phone at his desk rang.

"Hello, Blake speaking."

"This is Freeman," a gruff voice announced.

"Hello, Harv, what can I do for you?"

"I need a young woman, a small part. Can you set me up on that?" the studio producer inquired. "And by the way, thanks for putting Karla straight. She's behaving very well, now. I understand she's taken quite a liking to you. Well, how about the young girl? It's for a new scene in Karla's film."

"How young?"

"Oh, about twenty. Pretty—nothing hard or whorish. It's a small part, but you surely have a lot of young things willing to work hard and make friends."

"I know one woman who is very pretty, attractive, and I don't think Karla would bother you any. I think she'll fit. Dark-haired. Any problem?"

"No problem. She's simply to play an innocent who gets seduced. Then kills herself." Harv laughed. "Have to be pretty innocent and unstable for that!"

"There are some," Joe admitted. "Only thing, no funny stuff with this one."

"You know me, innocent as a babe." Coarse laughter came over the receiver.

"I mean it, Harv."

"Sure, sure. We'll treat her right. Nothing she wouldn't want to write home about. Okay, baby?"

"Okay," Joe offered a little hesitant. He knew the kind of man Freeman was and suddenly regretted having decided on Carol Fenton. This one would be free of the agency. The idea had popped into his mind without any mental consideration. All at once he was thinking about her, and here was a producer willing to give an unknown a break. The trouble with Harv Freeman was the fact that he usually made the young beginner pay heavily for any part in his movies. But, maybe, this would be different. Harv wouldn't risk getting in trouble with the agency, especially since Karla wasn't giving him any trouble.

Joe sat thinking about Carol, wondering why he was taking the chance of seeing her at all. It could be dangerous; especially after Karla's remarks the night before.

Again the phone rang, this time it was a woman's voice. Immediately he recognized Karla.

"Hello, darling, how is my love doing today, after last night?"

"Tired."

"Think you could stand another session tonight?"

76

"No. Honestly."

"Come on, love, you gotta be kissing me all over again. What'll I do all by my little self?"

"Get a little beauty sleep for the shooting tomorrow morning."

"I'm beautiful enough, and you know it," she laughed a little stiltedly. "I want you, love. You make me want you more than just once a week. That's not enough for this hungry girl!"

"Honest, I have some important matters to take care of tonight. It's impossible. Anyway, I want to turn in early for my own beauty sleep." The last thing he wanted was to be even a million yards near that woman. He felt the burn of guilt every time he thought of her. Especially because she was so hot to be with. She was an amazing mixed bag. And he could take just so much without having time to cleanse himself.

"I'll not beg, but I can't promise I'll be feeling very well tomorrow."

"Don't be foolish. You'll feel fine after a hot shower and a long sleep."

"A hot shower is nothing like a hot man." She hesitated, then said, "Okay...this time around. It was a little rough for you, I guess. Better give you time to lick your wounds and then you can come over tomorrow to take...care of me." She laughed again, a little forced this time. "You get a good night's rest, Joe, 'cause little me is going to want a real live party over the weekend. It'll be Friday and no studio work on Saturday for me. We might go someplace out of town. What do you think?"

"Nothing." His word was a little harsh. But she was pushing matters; and that was the last thing he wanted.

"You better think a lot about it. Like I said, I want you more than once a week, love. I need your doctoring! You are the drink my body craves! Hot and wild. I simply can't get enough of it, luv. Tonight I might have to call up a sub to fill in for you. It'll leave me hungry, thirsty; but better than starving from thirst! So...tomorrow for sure! Come up with something great."

"I don't know, Karla..." he offered, desperately trying

to find some way out of her demanding weekend party offer.

"What could be more important than servicing your main Star Bitch?" she laughed, rather harshly.

"You aren't the only client we—"

"I'm the only one you have to worry about, luv!"

"Christ!" exploded. "What do you expect?"

"Just a lotta lovin', luv. And, quite frankly, I didn't like that tone in your. voice, dearie." She was super sweet, now. "How about Ventura for the night and day, day and night? I know a wonderful place. Okay? It's settled."

The receiver went dead.

Joe cursed inwardly, stood and then left the office, heading for his father's. Without waiting to be announced, he barged past the secretary and then into the huge, plush office with its wall to wall book cases filled with movie scripts.

A squat, balding man with kindly eyes sat behind the large oak desk, reading a script. He looked up over his horn-rimmed glasses, then frowned.

"I wasn't to be bothered for anyone. That means you, too, Joey."

"I want to get off this Karla Kane account," he announced with some force.

"What the problem?" his father inquired, putting the script on the desk, taking off his glasses and leaning forward. "Is she too much a woman for you?"

Joe felt suddenly naked. It was difficult as hell to talk about sex with the man. Yet Old Man Blake, as they called him in the office, was not in the least embarrassed. "Well, son, is that the trouble?"

"You could put it that way," he managed, sitting in the large overstuffed leather chair opposite his father. "She's too much for any man."

"Who would you suggest?"

He studied his father's probing eyes. The heavy face was lined with serious concern.

"I'm no man's fool, son, and I won't pull my punches," the older man announced, relaxing back in his large chair. "The facts are simple enough. Her contract here is due for renewal in three months. We have to keep her happy. She'd blow the whole thing wide. Now, to be quite frank and seri-

78

ous about this matter, I had a talk with her the other day—just to make sure...that things were working out well." he added with a wave of his thick hand. "Don't get all stuffy about this, son. I'm running a business. You're doing fine here. But I have to know for certain." He leaned forward, placing his glasses on a hawk nose. "Can I be honest with you?"

Joe shrugged, shifted restlessly in the chair. He felt something like a stranger with his father. For years they had been almost strangers. Ever since his mother died eight years back, and his father remarried, a girl half his age, the gap had widened.

"Karla called me first—weeks ago—mentioned you in no uncertain terms, saying she'd like to have you handling her account. I'm not blind. I know what she is—and I knew what she was after. So...I did the only thing I could. So...like I said, I talked to her after the first meeting a few weeks back. She said you were everything she had hoped for and then some. She told me that everything would be just fine just so long as you continued to be nice to her. So...there you are, son. You continue to be...nice to her in every way. I know she can be very demanding. But hell, what's wrong with a little demanding from a star?"

A serious silence fell between the two of them, then his father said: "Karla's the type of woman you need right now...especially after what happened with Clara. I know what you've been through. I think something up there," he pointed to the heavens, "watches over us and lets things happen to make life a little easier at times of need. You gotta get out of yourself and stop just drifting. Play along with her, Joey. She'll make a man out of you."

Joe stiffened. They had never seen eye-to-eye about life. His father liked a more bitchy type of woman—since his first wife's death. His father also slept out on his present wife; something that Joe did not go along with. He believed that in marriage it was either park it or drive it—but no cheating.

He sighed. Standing, Joe said: "If that's the way it is..."

"That's the way. Stick to her. It won't kill you—and once the contract is signed...and...to be honest, Karla will tire even of you. She'd tire of a Greek God. That's the kind of woman she is. She uses up lovers and then goes on to the next one. It won't kill you, son. It'll make a man out of you. Just keep a stiff lower…you know what! Just what you need to forget Clara—a terrible event, I understand. But grow up, son!"

"Forgetting that that was done a long time ago," he said bitterly.

"Forgetting nothing. You need something to take you out of that romantic dream you've been living."

"Like what?"

"Well…moping about."

"Talk to some of the girls, you'll think differently," Joe countered, immediately feeling like a stupid bastard. "I've been banging all that come my way. So…I don't need any Karla Kane to…quite frankly she uses a man like a piece of meat!"

He laughed. "Well, we use them, the same way! Turn around is fair play. And, anyway, she's some hot bitch in heat!"

"Christ!" was all Joe could think of to say. "I don't need her! There are plenty of other women around to smother my body into…"

His father blinked, then laughed. "That's not what I meant. That's kid stuff, too—at least the way you go about it. You're just escaping…not facing. You use the women, hopping about like a rabbit. Well, that's fine and dandy. But I'd much rather see you use sex as a powerful weapon to get what you want—that's what I'm talking about. Karla uses her body as a weapon—and most of the people around the industry who are smart learn to use it like a weapon. Any woman or man can supply sex…nothing strange or supernatural about it. But…when you can look at sex as a weapon to get things—that's different. That's the difference between a tramp and a woman who becomes a star. The star knows who to sleep with, how to go about it, and how to take advantage of the fact. They get their kicks other ways…with guys like you! Now you learn the tricks, and you'll make a sharp agent. We have to know the tricks to teach the many young things that pass through our offices. You have to understand what makes people tick. Understand Karla—and

any woman you come along with—and you will begin to understand how to lead women in the right direction. Never
forget, there will be times when you'll be told by a producer,
'If she'll sleep with me, I'll give her the part.' You have to
decide if the woman knows how to make him keep the promise, and if he means to keep it, and then you have to advise
the girl. That kind of thing happens every day. We feed a lot
of young things to people like Larry Bershaw. He feeds the
savages of the town with hot bodies to toy with. But with
serious clients…well…you have to protect them from being
used as whores and then thrown aside. Understand that, son,
and you'll be a long way in getting ahead in the business."

With that the older man picked up the script, thus ending
the interview.

STAR BITCH, BY CHARLES NUETZEL

Chapter Ten

Carol Fenton felt a thrill as she stepped out of her car to see Joe Blake pacing back and forth in front of her apartment house.

"Hello," he greeted. "Thanks for phoning the office and telling my secretary your address."

She laughed happily. "I couldn't very well give it to you...before. Karla was right in front of me, and I was terribly frightened she would guess what was really happening."

As Carol came up to his side, Joe took her arm and the contact was surprisingly pleasant. Ever since the lunch together she had thought a lot about him. Last night her dreams had been erotically embarrassing to her; though hardly undesirable.

"I have some good news for you, Carol," he said as she led the way to her apartment door.

"Oh, what kind?" She fitted the key into the lock. They stepped into the darkened living room, and she flipped on the light. "Mix yourself a drink—in the kitchen...me too...while I fix myself up."

"You look simply delightful as you are," he announced. "Okay...I'll tell you all about it over the cocktails. What do you have?"

"Scotch...and Gordon's Gin. A friend brought the gin. I've been told that one should only use English gins. Another friend told me that." She felt wicked saying those things, for they weren't quite true, yet she felt the irresistible urge to make him think he wasn't the only man in her life. "I'll be right back. Make them strong martinis."

"Fine. That suits me just fine," he announced, finding his way into the kitchen.

She moved into the bedroom and closed the door. Carol slipped out of the blouse and skirt and then admired herself in the mirror. She had a very healthy figure, the kind that Playboy magazine liked to feature in its center spread. Her breasts her well formed, bouncy would be the right word. She had nice nipples, not too large, pert, might be a correct description, she thought, taking off her bra and then slipping out of her panties.

Moving to the bathroom, which had a private door from the bedroom, Carol turned on the shower, waited for the water to get warm, and then, after placing a cap over her jet black hair, stepped under the warm water.

An almost wild tingle of erotic pleasure teased over her as the needle spray surged forcefully down on her body.

A flush moved at Carol's cheeks. Never before had she been so excited about a date. It was so strange.

But, then, never before had she felt any natural temptation to let a man make love to her at the first possible moment. Maybe it was just a part of growing up, or being by herself for the first time in life—maybe she needed an adventure. Or was it simply that the right man hadn't come along up until now?

Those thoughts teased her, while at the same time her body was wondering what it must feel like to have a man captured in her.

A wonderful shiver attacked Carol; along with a sharp sense of embarrassment.

All her life at home she'd believed that sex should be saved for marriage, but now, trying to get into show-business, turning twenty-three in November—only months away—and still a virgin, everything seemed different. She was probably the last virgin she knew. All the girls in college had known at least one affair. She'd been a prude.

The last couple of weeks, living in this apartment, spending the long hours of night alone without companionship of any kind, Carol had begun to learn a basic fact of life: one couldn't stand it all alone—one needed somebody. And most men just weren't satisfied in merely holding hands, kissing, necking and petting. At least, not the ones who were really interesting.

84

Stepping out of the shower, Carol observed her body again in the tall mirror pinned to the door. It was probably a crime for that body to still be untouched by a man's.

She shrugged off the thought. Several times in the past she had toyed with the idea of going all the way with some date, but in the end had shied from letting it happen.

Was there something wrong with her? she wondered. *Was it because she didn't have any strong sexual drives?*

The thought terrified her. Then Carol argued, while pulling out a neat, form-fitting cocktail dress, *why did she tingle so when near Joe Blake?*

* * * * * * *

When Carol made her entrance into the living room, Joe felt sudden guilt at the thoughts that had tempted him while waiting. The sound of the shower had started them along very erotic levels. How interesting it would be to simply strip and walk in and join her. Of course it was impossible. With Karla that would be a natural. He didn't know Carol well enough, yet, to do such a thing; he simply wanted to know her that well, and as soon as possible. Now, with one glance at Carol Fenton, he felt shame.

Her hair fell loose around bare shoulders. The dress was black, open at the top to show off the top of her large bouncy breasts. The flare of her hips was hugged by the tight sheath of the skirt; the sleeves went to her forearms. There was everything about Carol, her manner of gracefully walking across the room, the sensual perfume that floated on the air around her, even the bright warm smile which played on her pouty lips, which seemed to offer: *here I am, all of me. Just for you.*

Yet there was something in the brightness of her dark, haunting eyes which screamed: *I'm a helpless woman, an innocent, don't take advantage of me.* That, he knew, was his imagination.

"Drinks ready?" she inquired, while slipping down beside him on the sofa.

"All ready," he grinned, handing her a very dry martini. He was sorry for having made them so dry. "Better be careful...a little on the strong side."

"Why be careful all your life, Joe?" she retorted with a bright smile, after taking a sip of the drink. "It tastes very good. I've been careful every day I've lived. Sometimes a girl wants to just live a little on the wild side, without worrying about tomorrow."

The invitation of her words was obvious enough; maybe too much so.

"Well, there's a time and place for everything, Carol." He unconsciously finished off the cocktail and then said, "I thought we might go the *Top of the Sunset*—then maybe a night club."

"That'd be wonderful," she admitted, lights shining in her eyes. She leaned close to him. "I was really surprised to hear from you today...though hardly unhappy about it."

An awkward silence followed, and Joe could see immediately she realized that her words might be too bold; too revealing.

"I'm glad." Suddenly he wanted to talk to Carol, but didn't exactly know what about. It was more the urge to just speak about all the problems which were annoying him every day. Abruptly he said: "I was talking to my father today about getting out of the...well, not having to handle Karla."

Carol looked away. After taking a strong swallow of her drink, she stated, "I thought you were...well, getting along with her."

"Would it surprise you, Carol, if I said that...I have no choice?"

"Who would want one?" Immediately she added, "I mean, wouldn't almost any man want to be in your position?"

"I guess so...but—damn it all...nothing. Forget it." After a moment he claimed: "Sometimes I wonder if I'm cut out for this kind of job."

She turned, faced him, and asked in a level, serious voice: "Why stay?"

"Well, dad wanted it that way so..."

"That sounds rather strange, Joe. You're a grown man. Surely you don't let your father—"

"Run me? No. Not exactly. Just that the agency seemed

86

a natural. Out of college, out of the army, and why shouldn't I? There are a lot of guys my age struggling to even get a break...here I am, handling an important account. But..."

"Maybe you should be on your own. I never did believe it was good for father and son to work together."

"What makes you say that?"

"Just...well, for myself, I wanted to be out on my own, totally—like I told you before. If I was a man I don't think I'd like the idea of working for my father." She shrugged, and her breasts moved easily against the neckline.

How attractive she is, he thought, pleased at the sight.

It would be so easy to seduce Carol, he was sure of that; surer of it than anything in the world. He'd known a lot of young girls who came on strong like her, inexperienced, who fell for a ready, smooth line. She wanted to grow up fast, but was afraid. All she needed was some guy to approach it in the right way.

Joe shrugged the thought out of his mind. Like he had said: there was a time and place.

"Let's go have something to eat. I don't know about you, but I'm starved, and the martini sparked a grand desire to eat."

But his eyes were almost paralyzed to her face and figure and the thoughts which whirled through his mind must have been written on his face for Carol flushed, stood, said in a throaty voice, "I guess you're right."

The meaning behind her words were as obvious as the sudden desire that throbbed at his temples.

"I think," Carol said huskily, "we had better get out of here. Before...something unseemly happens!"

Suddenly he was standing, reaching for her. She came quickly into his arms, but held back, away from his lips.

"Don't, Joe, please," she murmured, frowning.

The softness of her yielding body was almost too much to take. He could feel the quick reaction hardening every muscle in him to rigid steel. How he wanted her!

Slowly his hand slipped to his side. "I'm sorry."

She shrugged. "I guess you shouldn't be. Any girl likes...well the man to desire her...is that it?"

Her voice was so hesitant, so unsure, that Joe felt a sudden pang to protect her, to gently pull that dear form close to his, saying that nothing would ever hurt or harm her as long as he was around. He wanted to literally envelope her in a total embrace—like a surrounding shield. And at the same time every nerve wanted to violate her lush, lovely body.

Instead, he shrugged. "Okay, my young lady, off we go to feast on a big healthy steak—or anything your heart desires."

She gathered her purse and the two of them left without another word.

Chapter Eleven

As Carol Fenton was waiting in the outer office of Harv Freeman, a sense of tension pushed up through her. Up until now she had been thinking more about Joe Blake, and their date last night, than anything else. He had forgotten to tell her about the interview until they had parked outside her apartment. After dinner they had spent a wonderful evening merely sitting at a cocktail lounge, talking. It was the most delightful date she had ever experienced. Her feelings for Joe Blake, Carol realized, were already showing alarming signs of a crush; it could hardly be more than that. One didn't fall in love at first site; that was romantic fantasy offered up in films. Adults weren't that stupid.

Throughout the evening, Joe had dropped little hints, obviously unconscious, of being highly unhappy with his job. The promised night-clubbing had never come about, because he had seemed more in the mood to talk than anything else, and she was more than willing to listen. When they sat outside her apartment, she had moved close to him, and his arm had slipped around her shoulder. All the time she was trying to think of some way to invite him up for a nightcap. What might happen after that was something she actually looked forward to. She actually wanted intimacy with him. Never before had a man driven her to such a peak of determination. This was the guy she wanted to have as her first lover; it was as simple as that. Carol didn't even debate that conclusion; it was a fact she accepted with open arms.

But the words of invitation would not come. She merely didn't know how to sat them without looking cheap.

She turned around and slipped her arms around his neck and for the first time they had kissed. It all happened too quickly, on impulse, that she was not really aware of being the aggressor. His lips were warm and soft under hers, but in such a mannish, exciting way. When she opened her mouth to his kiss, he seemed to hesitate, then all at once he was crushing her form against his, tongue entering her mouth deep, creating a wild excitement she had never before experienced.

Then all at once he'd gently pushed her back at arm's distance.

"Carol, let's not play little children's games," he told her, and for a moment she believed he was going to suggest they go someplace and spend the night together. "You're too exciting...and I don't want to take advantage of you. Not right now. Okay?"

It was such a startling, unexpected statement that Carol could only stare at him, unable to reply. She wasn't quite sure how to take it; as a rebuff or something else.

"I mean it, Carol. Just do us both a favor and not push it—I don't think I could resist...control myself." Then, abruptly, as if changing the subject on purpose, he exclaimed, "I forgot all about the interview."

"What interview?"

When he explained about Harv Freeman looking for a young actress to play a part in Karla Kane's movie, all thoughts lifted away from the sensual and moved to the stunned sensational.

"You're kidding?" she fairly screamed in delight.

"Why not? You said you wanted a part in the movies, and now here's your chance. Just one warning about Harv...he's on the make for every girl who comes onto the lot." He stared seriously at her for a moment, "I'd hate to think you felt it necessary to..."

"How could you?" she countered, flushing at the very thought.

"Just don't think you have to let him take any—and I mean any—liberties. It's not necessary. Even if that's why he really wants to see you...he plays this kind of game with all the young women who might be influenced by his power to fire and hire. Walk on though it might be, he'll want to pass on you before handing over the part. That's Harv. He's

90

a hand-on, independent producer. And usually wants them on a woman's...well you fill in the blanks. But don't bite. Just go to the studio tomorrow—read for the part—and if you have any talent, he'll hire you. Nothing more than that." Then with that last remark, he slipped out of the car. "Which means its past three, and you'll need some rest...I shouldn't have kept you out this long as it is."

At the doorstep, she was sure he would kiss her good-night, but instead he merely shook hands awkwardly and then quickly turned, rushing to his car as if suddenly frightened of some invisible monster threatening to take possess his very soul.

And now here she was about to meet the Top Brass, Boss of Freeman Studios. The company offices were on a small studio lot near Sunset and Highland. She'd been told that Freeman rented his space and used it only when actually making a film. It was a small production company; but a wonderful start. Have Freeman had made some pretty impressive films. And this was the same studio which Karla was contracted to for her present film.

It all seemed too fantastic to believe. It was happening much too fast.

And her father had laughed at her in the beginning. After finding how serious she as about becoming an actress he'd said: "Carol, you don't know what its like to be alone in the world, you have no experience with life, you just can't imagine what you'll have to face. You're still a child." His last statement had been enough to drive a determination through her so strong that nothing would have stood in her way. "That's an adult's world and you have to be adult to fight it, on its terms." When she'd insisted that this was the only thing she wanted, and that she was merely asking one favor—the introduction to the right man—he'd nodded, sighed. "Okay, I'll see what can be done—but, to be truthful, I think you'll not last three months. Not in the Hollywood of truth and reality—which is nothing like the one in the glamour books and magazines."

These words rang in her ears as she gave a quick smile to the secretary who had told her to go on into the office. The door opened as she approached and a tall, big boned man with balding head and beady eyes moved toward her.

"Hello, sweetheart," he greeted, immediately placing a fatherly arm around her shoulders as he drew her into a large, plush office. The carpet was thick and soft, an off brown. There was a large coffee table to the right, in front of a sofa which she could imagine opened into a bed. The table had several ashtrays half filled with cigar and cigarette butts. Scripts were piled on a large metal desk in front of a broad window.

"Mr. Blake told me all about you, Carol—you don't mind me calling you that, do you?" His right hand accidentally pressed into her breast. "You are very lovely, dear."

He pushed her toward the sofa, and then after seating her there, stepped back, eyed her like a hawk. Under his gaze she felt like some kind of human meat viewed for market.

"Tell me how much experience you've had?" The question seemed to have some inner perverse meaning. "Any parts in professional productions? He didn't tell me much."

"To be honest, Mr. Freeman, I don't think he knows that much about me," she offered, opening her purse, taking out a cigarette. "Do you mind?"

"Of course not, make yourself at home. Anything you'd do in your own home—just anything." He was eyeing her bust line, then looking at her nylons as if he wanted to lick them off. She squirmed under the blatant stare. The bloody beast was so obvious.

"You say, he knows little about you?" Freeman inquired, taking a seat opposite her, an oily grin playing on his thick lips.

The idea of being forced into a bedroom scene with this man revolted Carol, and it was all she could do to hide that fact from her face. She forced a friendly smile. "I meant that he only knows I'm interested in acting, but we never went much further into that."

He nodded thoughtfully, stroked his mustache with thin, nervous fingers. "Well, why don't you tell me?"

She shifted restlessly, re-crossing her legs. His alert eyes caught every move she made. "I've studied acting with the Carlton Institute of Art, at UCLA, and done a couple of parts in...well, to be honest, amateur plays."

He nodded to each statement, then clapped his hands on his knees. "Well, that's not really the problem. The part is simple enough. Blake Enterprises is not in the habit of sending rank amateurs to us. I can depend on the agency. Now, tell me, have you ever read for a part in any film?"

"No," she admitted, frankly, feeling that she was losing points all the time. Yet he kept staring at her legs as if they fascinated him.

"Pick up one of the scripts there, and read a few lines."

He reached for one and tossed it to her. "Just open the script to any scene, and merely read any actor's lines you come to. It'll tell me enough."

It was a cold reading—blunt and one of the most difficult things for an actress or actor to do. Carol felt strangely detached as she opened the script. Without waiting, she let her eyes skim the top line of dialog and quickly read out loud, putting in the right amount of emotion which the lines themselves called for.

"'Well, dear, I don't care what you say, but I think that son of ours is in great trouble.'"

Moving to the next line, she toughened her voice, lowering it in pitch. *"'It's about time he learned what life's all about. So he gets a little pushed. Well life pushes people around...I got pushed when I was a young man, It wasn't easy building the business—from nothing. Just me and sweat. He has to learn that.'"*

She looked up at Freeman, unable to resist an ad-lib of her own, saying in the woman's voice:

"'But, dear, he's only two months old. Don't you think that's a little young to join the army?'"

Freeman burst out laughing, pounding his fists against the table. "I'd never expected that," he announced after sobering up. "Young lady, you show a sparkling wit. So few actresses have that ability to poke fun."

He stood, moved down beside her, and placed a heavy hand on her leg. He patted her thigh. It was meant to be sensual. She felt cold and clammy.

"Do I get the part?" she inquired, staring unemotionally into the man's eyes.

His face hardened. The lips drew thin across his large

teeth. "What's with you, girl?"

His hand remained on her thigh, high up, the fingers stiffened.

"Nothing. I would just like to know. A natural question, don't you think?" She looked down at his hand, not making any attempt to hide her dislike to it being where it was.

It didn't move. "A woman with as much wit as you've displayed shouldn't be so damned silly," he snapped, angrily. "With the part comes some responsibilities, and you haven't revealed any talents to take directions!"

Abruptly he stood. "Now, I won't beat around the bush, young lady. My time is money. How do I know if you can act? You read well, that's all. Can you walk? Can you put on a magnetic sexual attitude? The part we have in mind is that of a young woman, seduced, who then kills herself afterwards. Can you play that kind of woman?"

A chill ran down her spine. "Why not?"

"Let's see." He moved to his desk, pushed aside several scripts, and then picked up a fat one, opened it to a page and then came back to her side. "Now," he said, "Let's act the part out."

The chill became ice that paralyzed Carol. How far would he want to play it out?

"The lines are simple enough. All you have to remember is, 'But, Johnny, I love you, doesn't that mean anything to you.' If you want, ad-lib any bit that seems intelligent. I'll play the young man. I think you can use your imagination a little about that."

He placed an arm around her shoulders, drew her close. "Relax, Carol. Try playing a young woman in love—the guy you love is going to pull every trick in the book on you—and in the end, you'll have yourself all boxed up, unable to resist. It's an adult part, and it'll be an innocent being seduced for the first time. I assume you can imagine how the girl might feel."

Carol felt rigid, but forced her thoughts on the concept of the young woman she was supposed to be playing. It wouldn't be hard to appear slightly frightened.

"Connie, you know I love you...there's never been a girl like you before. Don't punish me simply because...because

94

I'm not...well, free of responsibilities," he said in a smooth, though corny actor's voice, hugging her closer. "After all, we're adults...both over twenty-one. Why don't you grow up? Why do you hobble yourself with all this middle-class morality? You'll just be unhappy because of it."

"But, Johnny, I love you, doesn't that mean anything at all to you?" she countered, frantically pressing against his chest with her right hand. The fear was real. Suddenly she knew how helpless she might be in the man's grasp.

"If you loved me, you wouldn't deny me anything."

Then as he attempted to draw her lips to his, Carol jerked out of his grasp, determined not to allow him any further rights.

"This has gone on far enough!" she snapped, honest anger touching her voice.

Obviously not aware that she was serious, Harv Freeman grabbed at her, his eyes passionate, lustful like those of a silent film actor about to attack the pretty young innocent. "Either you grow up and start acting like a woman or we're through!"

Carol immediately forced herself to ad-lib a line, to turn her honest emotions into the little play—what made her realize how important this was, she never quite remembered.

"Don't you care, Johnny, about how I'd feel? Don't you ever think about anybody except yourself? Can't you realize that some girls think of love as something special?"

Carol realized that the scene was a mock-seduction for Harv the man on the make. He was serious about stripping her naked and possessing her in the flesh—no holds barred. The man was blatant ass.

He laughed, the sound was bitter. "There's nothing special about love except with the right person. When it's right, it would be wrong to deny it. Look at us, here we are, alone, supposed to be in love—and you're putting up old fashioned ideas to protect—what? In a modern world like this, everybody knows the score, except you. I told you I love you, what more do you want?"

Carol shook her head, "Do you really believe a girl would fall for that line?"

Now it was difficult to tell if he was playing the part any

longer. They had gone into a freeform ad-lib; but continually within the framework of a fictional plot—even while the man was bluntly trying to truly seduce her. Now it was obvious that both of them were lost somewhere between reality and fiction.

He coughed, glanced at the script, as if he'd been reading from it, looked up at her again, suddenly awkward.

"Many a girl has fallen for that kind of line—it's surprising how many. But it is not a line. It's the truth. And truth sometimes sounds rather fantastic when put into words."

"Very fantastic. I don't know who your script writer is—but a two-year-old child could see right through that material." She laughed, and then moved away from Freeman, determined to bring reality sharply into focus. "Was that part of the imaginary script, or something *you* ad-libbed?"

He stared at her for a long time, then finally said: "I don't know if you were acting or really playing a real part. But I'll tell you this—you have more guts and spirit than most women who come into this office." Then changing his tone of voice, as if aware of where things were not going, and added: "And you'd be surprised how many times I've used a gambit like this to get them willing to do what is politely stated as 'anything to get ahead'—though in the present case, I was honestly attempting to try you out for a part which just accidentally happens to be in the film." He stood, moved behind his desk, sat down. "You're right, of course, no woman in her right mind would believe those words—but women in love will believe anything a man tells them. A young woman trying to get a break in films will do anything to please those who might give her a part. You have guts not playing along with the gag. Most women do! If they want the part, that is…"

"Mr. Blake told me it wasn't necessary," she announced, blandly. "I assume he's right!"

"Why that dirty young man!" Freeman growled half serious. "I bet if he hadn't, you would have."

"I'm afraid not! Like the girl in the film—the part—I might have killed myself afterwards," she countered, only half kidding. "Well, maybe not myself…maybe just the studio boss!"

She let that hang in mid-air, with only a light twisted smile on her lips.

He gave her a double take, then grinned. "I almost believe you would."

They both laughed, then he said, "Have my secretary give you one of the scripts, read up on the part—it'll be penciled in—and come back next Monday and we'll give you a screen test. If that looks good, and I see no reason why it shouldn't, I'll let you have the part. Okay?"

Like a robot she nodded, unable to speak.

"Now, run along, I'm an important man, and have a lot of things to do."

As she started out of the room, she heard him mutter: "What a woman…real guts!"

STAR BITCH, BY CHARLES NUETZEL

Chapter Twelve

The minute they arrived at the hotel, checked into their room, Karla announced: "I want to take a shower—you better, too. It's been a long day, and a long ride."

They were at a beachside hotel, facing the ocean. Night played romantically on the world, sparkling stars looked down from a clear heaven.

Karla slipped immediately out of her dress, stood before him, hands on hips. "Come on, love, I said we were going to take a shower. Don't you get the message? This Star Bitch want you to simply ravish her in every way!"

He looked at her trim figure, so lovely for any woman at any age, and felt a pang of restless nervousness. All the way up to Ventura, Joe had wanted to turn around, drive home, and tell Karla it was quits, that he just couldn't go on with this charade. But he realized there was no way out. He felt like a trapped slave, captured and being ordered to please the mistress of lust, regardless, or his head would be lopped off.

"How about a drink?" he suggested, a little frightened that she might object and he couldn't get himself drunk enough to live out this week-end with a woman who was now beginning to slightly disgust him. It was strange, because Karla was the fantasy of so many young men across the world. Fans hungered for her body in their sexual dreams. And here she was, demanding him to ravish her for a whole weekend. What was more unnerving was the fact that in her arms it was impossible not to enjoy every moment of the ravishing.

Yet he desperately wanted out; felt trapped. And sick at the whole scene; especially his own churning desire for her passion hungry body. She was an exhausting mixed bag. It

99

was raw sex; nothing more. Under any other circumstance it might have been a wonderful experience; an ideal situation. Hot sex with a lusting famous star, no holds barred, no strings. Expect for the string she held in her tight claws. She had total power over him. She was a puppet-mistress pulling all the strings, playing him like a boy toy to use, abuse and then, when bored, kicked out on his ass. Just exactly like the casting couchers used their power over young actors wanting parts and willing to do anything in order to get ahead in the business. Power brokers used and abused people to be crushed helpless in their arms. A dirty business. A nasty situation when on the short end of the stick. She swung the whip and it was snapping right across his back. Hot as Karla might be, she was in total control. Brutalizing power was in her hand and that made him a sexual slave to the woman's demands. She wanted him totally submissive to her will. That was her game. Sex, raw, down and dirty, and no emotional attachments. And nothing beyond that.

And he wanted a lot more. But not with her! Yet there was no way out.

If it was anybody's but his father's agency he would have told the boss to shove it deep. But what should he say to his own father?

A part of his mind rebelled from all that hesitation, all that annoyance. That part of him was reacting to her body, to the promise of total erotic pleasure it was offering, demanding, expecting, and willing to give in an endless banquet of sex-games.

"Want a drink?" he asked, again.

"Why not, love?" She flashed him a quick smile. Her hands removed the bra in one swift motion as she said, "Fix me a strong one."

She shivered slightly and her breasts responded, almost teasingly trembling. He couldn't get his eyes off the nipples, so pert, erect.

"Like what you see, hon?" she murmured, pleased. "Well, I love the way you respond. Just love it! So down and dirty!" Her eyes were feasting on his groin which was already hurting hard. "My, you sure do get big, don't you?"

She grinned in delight. "Just love it when a man gets

100

so…well developed at the sight of my boobs! My titties just hurt like that does…down there…" Her hand made a clawing action, as if grabbing at him. "My, how I have been wanting that!"

She just stood there staring at him, wanton temptation.

He opened the travel bag which held two bottles of scotch. The way he was feeling right now he could have downed both,

While he was opening the first bottle, Karla came up behind him and crushed her breasts against his back. "That feels good. I can't wait to know the hot feel of you, love. Last night I thought I'd go mad. Would you believe me if I said that all I could think about was what we could do here together? It made me tingle all inside, deep inside until I couldn't stand it. Had to take two sleeping pills to escape the pain."

Her fingers stroked his chest, then gliding downwards, teasing, then slowly moved upwards across his chest again, into his shoulders.

"What's wrong, love," she demanded, digging long sharp nails into his flesh, "aren't you just dying to get into me…with all that…wonderful male…beastie? You don't wanna get all drunk, now do you? Gotta keep yourself sober and real wild…I know you like little Karla! Tell me. Tell me how much you love it with me! I want to hear the word coming from your lips. You do love me, don't you?"

She wasn't making sense.

"Come on, Karla…"

"You didn't answer me. Tell me how much you love me, Joe, I want to hear it from your own lips."

Twisting around, he stared at her, unable to believe the demand. "What the hell's love have to do with us?"

"Tell me you love me, Joe!" Her voice was threatening.

"Are you kidding?" He held the bottle almost like a weapon and realized how much he wanted to smash it into her face.

"Say you love me, Joe," she demanded again. "I want to hear it, *right now.*"

"What difference does it make? You have a great body. Isn't that enough?" Irritation was so thick on his voice that it

101

amazed himself. "I love your body. Is that want you want to hear?"

"Not even close!" she snapped, glaring at him. "I want you to love me!"

"Come on, Karla. Be reasonable. This isn't love—its sex on demand!"

"What's that mean?" she almost screamed, furious.

"You demand and I service you. That's what it means. Nothing more!"

"What's with you?" Her fingers clawed, clutched his shoulders, cruel and hard.

"Come on, be reasonable."

"I want to hear it!"

"Well you aren't going to. I won't lie to you!" he announced, determined to draw a desperate line. She could demand him as a sexual toy, but not expect lies concerning emotional statements. "You're fantastic in bed. But I don't love you. So stop that crap! Use me if you must, but don't try wrapping it in some kind of fancy romantic fantasy. Get real!"

"Damn you! You pig! You filthy stud!" she exploded, swinging a right at his face.

Joe ducked just in time, grabbed her arm, and then shoved her down on the double bed. "Don't do that again."

For a long time she glared up at him, then a slight smiled curled her lips. Suddenly it was obvious that she'd enjoyed being pushed, dominated.

"What's wrong with you, Joe?" she cooed, suddenly changing her tack. "You're always so serious. I can't understand you. I'm sorry about...trying to hit you...but you sounded so...well, let's forget that. But, please, don't you love me a little bit?" There was a pleading quality to her voice. She lay there, breasts naked, panties so small and lacy that it was almost as if they didn't exist.

"What's all this love, anyway? I didn't think you dealt in love, Karla," he stated unemotionally, starting for the glasses on the dresser. Slipping them out of their paper casings, he filled them almost all the way with straight scotch. "I thought you only wanted sex parties. Not love!"

"We all want love, don't we? To feel needed as a human

102

being; not just some...object! We want to be admired, de-sired and certainly loved for what we are. What's wrong with that?" she inquired conversationally, as he handed her one of the glasses. "God, that's a stiff jolt."

"We need a stiff jolt, I think."

"Doesn't everybody need love, Joe?" she asked as he took a large swallow of the scotch.

It was some moments before he answered. She waited, just staring up at him.

"I guess so," he said absently, thinking suddenly about Carol Fenton. There was a girl who could make him need and want love. He shook off the thought. Ever since their date he'd been teased by thoughts of love. He needed a love involvement like a hole in the head. Damned Carol. Damned Karla.

He turned his attention once more towards the woman. Maybe this was just what he needed. Forget her demands, her power plays and just enjoy that great body, her passion, her lush love-making.

"Maybe you're right," he muttered, letting his eyes sweep over her body. "You're sure one hell of a sexy broad!"

"I'm a Star Bitch in heat. Right?" she laughed.

"Just say you're a hot female," he managed, wanting to leave it at that. There was nothing he could do other than make the most of the weekend, enjoy her on a physical level and forget the rest. Escape totally within her demanding embrace. "A very hot lady!"

"Well, thank you. At least that's better than nothing. I suppose. A woman likes to be wanted, needed, desired, and considered a hot whore in bed! Makes me shiver thinking that. Believing a man considers me hot stuff! But...well, sometimes I want even more than that. I'm no different from other women, Joe. I might look different—it might seem dif-ferent—and I might act different—but I want to be loved, too. I wouldn't be human if I didn't want love." She was chattering, and the sound of her voice became distant. "So what's wrong in wanting the man you're loving it up with to love you at least a little bit? Why shouldn't I want your love? You're terribly good in bed. I like all your muscles. I think I love you a bit. After all, its impossible to be as intimate as the two of us without feeling some kind of emotional reaction. Some attachment beyond pure, raw sexual worship. And I do worship your big...well, your big *everything!*"

She stood, moved to him, her breasts touched his chest, the nipples like little points pressing through the shirt. "Yes, come to think of it, I do feel a great emotional reaction towards you. Very strong. Strong as hell. I guess you might say I'm in love. How could I help myself—after what you do to me? I just love you for it. Can't you love me a little in return for what I do to you?"

Joe felt more that his emotional reaction was pure hatred. But the pleading and somewhat desperate look in Karla's eyes warned him.

"How could a man not love Karla Kane? Especially after what we've experienced?" he inquired. But the question had far deeper meaning for him than it suggested to her. The fact was that he hated her guts with such a violence that it was almost impossible to keep from hitting her again and again until she screamed for him to stop, leave her forever. But her reaction would probably be just the opposite. And, anyway, there was the responsibility to his father and the agency. She was that important.

And very hot. At least he had to hand her that! A wild flame that burned into anything she touched. And she was touching him, very intimately.

Her breasts rubbed against him, the nipples now hard. She slipped her arms about his neck. "I'm on fire for you, Joe. Real blistering all over. My nerves hurt so much to feel you taking me. Feel you deep inside, just stirring away, like you wanted to turn me into butter. Oh, I'm feeling like melting all over you. Can't we please...stop all this talk. Let's take a shower. We might have a little fun in there."

She was right. If he had enough liquor it wouldn't matter much who she was. She'd be just a body. Nothing more.

"We'll have a lot of fun. You'd be surprise how much fun...real fun." Her hand touched him teasingly. "Come on, love, put down the drink, get undressed." Her fingers slipped under his belt. "I want what you have under all that...clothing. I can't wait to get my hands on you. Wrap my fingers

104

around you, feeling all that wonderful, powerful need for me...oh, hon, I'm sick with wanting!"

"Hell, I'll undress myself," he cried, pulling away.

Her fingers held his belt, pulled him toward her. "I'll undress you, love. That's half the fun. You just lap up your drink and I'll show you how a man should be undressed."

With that her fingers undid his belt buckle.

STAR BITCH, BY CHARLES NUETZEL

Chapter Thirteen

Karla fairly pushed Joe into the shower, then squeezed in beside him. The water was slightly hot, but the pressure of her damp body against his was even hotter, especially after the way she'd undressed him. His mind was now totally obsessed with her love-making. No man would be able to think of anything other than total sex games after taking the kind of punishment Karla had dealt out a few moments before.

Her form was pressed flush against his, and she circled his neck with slender arms, drawing her lips up under his.

"See what I mean, love?" she murmured, after running her tongue along his lips.

The hotness of her thighs drove his body to a new peak of need. But how the hell could anything be done in the cramped shower to relieve that need was beyond his imagination to figure out.

"Kiss me deep, love," she demanded, squirming.

Then her mouth opened and there was nothing but to drive his tongue into the well of her offering lips that closed around his tongue, holding it clasped in its soft, moist captivity.

The mixture of scotch, hot spraying water and the dampness of her naked flesh almost glued to his, built the surging power of lusting passion to a raw peak.

His right hand surged hard against her breast, palming the nipple until it was like soft steel. She moaned, bit hard on his tongue until it hurt. The pain caused him to squeeze at her breast, clutching in tension. Her hips squirmed hotly trembling against him.

As the kiss broke, Karla moaned. "Joe...Joe, that was good, delicious. Squeeze it hard again, hurt me so much I

107

could scream."

Her ankles wrapped around his calves, and it seemed as if he were supporting her whole body in his arms. Then her hips moved flush against him, only to slip away and then back again. It drove him wild.

"Hurt me, Joe. Hurt me deliciously." Her eyes were half-lidded, her lush mouth parted, teeth clasped tight together.

"Hurt me, damn you!" she screamed, clawing at his back, nails ripping at the muscles and flesh as if attempting to part them from one another.

"Damn it!" he cursed, and suddenly he wanted to hurt her. His fingers clawed at soft shoulders, squeezed with every ounce of strength.

She softly sobbed, moaned, and then suddenly went wild, like a raging beast.

"Now. Now!" she screamed, face contorted with emotion. "Now...*now!*"

Her body was whipping against his, frantically attempting a union which seemed impossible. Then suddenly she had captured him totally.

She convulsed like a dying animal, speared through the heart. Her hands were clawing, clawing his back as racking moans gushed from her wide open mouth.

"Do...something!" she screamed.

There was nothing he could do. The contorted passion on her face, the demanding commands, had iced his mind, though nerves still reacted to the raw sensual force of this heated woman who didn't seem to be able to get enough of a man.

Like a savage she shoved his body away, pushed him out of the shower.

"You bastard!" she cried, coming out like a tigress. "Now...now do it right!" Hands grabbed him, and then the two of them all but fell to the floor. Her body positioned itself as an open offering, thighs parted wide.

Under the circumstances there was nothing he could do but satisfy their mutual lusts. In one swift moment he entered her and she screamed in ecstasy.

108

* * * * * * *

Karla snapped the cigarette into her mouth, looked out the window, picked up a lighter, lit the cigarette and then reached for the glass of scotch of the end table next to the chair.

Her body ached from the long hours of loving she'd experienced with Joe Blake. She rubbed her naked breasts, feeling a new surge of strength and need touch her. She wanted him right now. The minute he returned from getting the bottle of whiskey from the bar, she'd demand that he screw her royally.

Such a strong, muscular body. How she loved that body of his. How she was turned on by that violence he flooded over her. She liked it better with Joe Blake than any man she'd ever met before in her life.

"I'm in love," she murmured almost with a sigh. "I've never been so much in love."

The thought that Joe Blake might not feel the same way sent a stabbing chill through Karla. That was one thing she could not stand. No man had ever turned Karla down. What she'd gone after she'd always won.

The idea of Joe desiring some other woman, touching a woman other than herself, created a flood of sudden violent emotion through her. She could not consider that. Ever since she'd met Joe, her body had been hot for him alone. He was like some Greek God. So tall, broad shouldered, well muscled. He made her feel feminine all over at once.

The door to the room opened and then closed.

Karla turned to see Joe leaning back against the door, eyes glassy, a bottle of whiskey in his right hand. He stared at her as if not even seeing what was before him.

"Joe...what's wrong?"

"Nothing. Just a little drunk, that's all."

"Don't booze it up too much, love, I gotta lot of energy which needs worked out of me. That studio is bumming me hard, and a bunch of pent up anxieties are needling me." She stood, moved toward him. As he attempted to walk around her, Karla grabbed out. Her hands closed on his shoulders. "What's wrong?"

The expression on his face was tired, irritated and a little bored.

She felt a pang of alarm. "What's wrong, love?"

"Can't you lay off it a little?" he complained, opening the bottle, ignoring her grip.

"Lay off what?"

"You know exactly what I mean? We've been at it all night...with just a little rest. A man can get a little pushed out of shape after too much of it." He shoved his way out of her grip, went to the glass which lay on the bedstand. Filling it, he took a large swallow of the straight liquor.

"Don't drink so much, love," she badgered, moving close, letting her hand rest on his thigh. "Why don't you just get undressed and—"

She moved her fingers higher.

"Damn it all, stop that!" he cursed, brushing her hand away. "Don't you know when to quit?"

"What's wrong with you, love?" she demanded. "You were fine half an hour ago."

"Well, now I'm tired." He lay back on the bed, putting his hands behind his neck, looking up at the ceiling.

"You had a nice rest, love. Come on, let's do it again. I'll make it good for you...believe me you'll like it." She leaned over him, kissed his cold lips. "Come on, give a girl a chance."

"What's with you, Karla? Don't you ever tire?" He glared up into her eyes with cold emotion.

"Are you kidding? Haven't you spent a weekend in a hotel room with a girl before? What you do, play cards? What's wrong with you, you some kind of queer?"

Joe Blake's right fist doubled up, started toward her face, then stopped short. "What's the use? you'd probably enjoy it."

Alarmed for the first time, Karla moved away from him. "What's wrong?"

"Nothing." He refused to look at her.

"Come on, out with it, You've changed. I demand that you tell me," She stood over him, hands on hips, naked to his gaze, which seemed to look totally through her.

"You want the truth, or some fantastic lie?" he spat out,

eyes meeting hers for the first time.

"What's wrong?"

"You. Everything. I've had it—up to here!" He chopped the air with his right hand, just above his neck.

"What have you had?" She ignored the alarming implication of his words.

"Forget it. I'm tired. Can't you understand?

"Even God was tired after six days—and he was creating the universe. We'll I'm only human and I'm tired after something like eight hours of it. Now, why don't you be a nice little girl and let her mechanical *stud* get some rest? Doesn't anything make you understand? Don't you get the message? Or are you too damned over-sexed? Is that it?"

A cold chill frosted Karla Kane. She started to say something, then changed her mind. "Okay, love, you get some beauty rest—I think you need it, you're acting damned ugly right now."

With that she gathered her clothes and began dressing. Several minutes later she stormed out of the room, went down the hall and to the south exit of the hotel. A short time later she was walking along the beach, trying to sort out her thoughts.

No man had ever talked to her in that manner and gotten away with it. For the first time she considered her reasons for taking it from Joe Blake. It was some time in coming, but finally she realized that for some fantastic reason she must really be in love with him. It was the only logical explanation.

Walking back to the hotel, Karla decided to play it different with Joe. Maybe he was right in that she had pushed him a little too much, too fast. Actually, Karla realized, he had been fantastic with her. The long night had been filled with fun and games that would have exhausted any man—or probably most women, too. But something was driving her beyond a normal point of need; she couldn't get enough of being close to Joe, feeling his muscles, his arms around her, his love-making, so violent and exciting.

As she stepped back into the hotel room, alarm choked her—Joe wasn't there.

Frantic, Karla rushed from the room, went to the cocktail lounge off the lobby. He wasn't there, either.

Going to the desk clerk, she asked: "Have you seen Mr. Blake come through the lobby? He's the man who came in with me."

The clerk looked at Karla Kane, made a double take, then grinned, pleased at seeing a movie star. "He was here...paid the bill for the weekend, then left."

"Left?" she screamed. Then embarrassment colored her cheeks. "What do you mean?"

"He said to give Miss Kane this message." The clerk held out an envelope.

She tore it open. The note was short, to the point.

"Need to be alone. Private problems. Sorry, Joe."

She looked up at the clerk, noticed the manner in which he was staring at her. A quick smile touched Karla's lips.

Abruptly she didn't give a damn about any sense of respectability.

"When are you off?" she quickly inquired.

"At two this afternoon." He looked puzzled. The man was in his early twenties, young, and she guessed unmarried. But that didn't make any difference to her. Even a married man could hardly turn Karla Kane down.

"Why don't you bring a bottle up to my room. I think I'll be needing it by then."

"By when?" he asked stupidly.

"When you are off. By two in the afternoon. Bring a bottle up and I'll give you a very handsome tip. A very...meaningful tip. One you'll never forget as long as you live. I can promise you that, in spades!"

She winked and then went to her room to get a little rest. She only had a couple of hours before the young clerk would be entering into one of the most fantastic afternoons he'd ever experienced—one which he would probably talk about for the rest of his life.

Chapter Fourteen

Joe Blake waited in the cocktail lounge, taking his first drink since Saturday afternoon. The last three days had been dry and sober ones, heavy with deep thought about his future. The one night in the hotel with Karla Kane had been enough to drive him to the point of cracking. He'd never wanted to run so much in his life. Since then he had made himself scarce, hiding out in a motel in Tarzana, trying hard to come to some solution about his life. When he had first come to work for his father, at the agency, everything had looked bright for his future. He was engaged to the young woman he'd gone to college with, marriage was a sure thing in another six months. They had picked out the kind of house they wanted, and even expected to build it on a lot his father had owned for some years; planning on buying the land before getting married. Then an auto accident had cut short all plans. After that, it had been a drunken escape from the hurt. Or so he had believed.

Now, Joe was beginning to doubt his motives. All his life he'd taken the easy way out. The job had been an easy way, marriage to Clara Henderson had been merely a logical step. After returning from the service, he enjoyed a quick spree with a number of women, started dating Clara again, and then asked her to marry him. Actually she had done most of the asking, in a way, by leading conversations around to marriage. They'd never had an affair; that was one weapon she'd used to push him into marriage.

Now, Joe wondered, could he actually have loved Clara very much if his emotional attention was so easily captured by another woman?

He looked at his watch. It was a little past seven. Carol

could be here in a few moments.

"Another martini," he ordered from the bartender.

"Meeting someone?" the white-haired man inquired conversationally.

"Supposed to." He smiled absently, then lit a cigarette.

He'd called Carol some thirty minutes ago. It had been impulsive, but an impulse that had built for three days. The office didn't know where he was, and he dreaded the thought of making an appearance. Karla probably had been furious.

The rustle of cloth attracted his attention.

"Can you order one of those for me?" Carol inquired taking the barstool next to him.

"I'm sorry about...well, asking you to come..."

"What? You want me to leave already?" she laughed, teasingly.

"No no. I mean, asking you to drive out—"

"Forget it." She was beaming; her face seemed so young and fresh.

"No, I should have picked you up and—"

"It was a nice drive."

Neither of them said anything until he had ordered her a martini.

"How'd you make out on the interview, Friday?"

"Oh, you don't know how happy I am about that. It all came at me so unexpectedly. There was a screen test yesterday and I understand it went real good. Mr. Freeman wants us to come in this Friday and sign a contract." The words gushed out so quickly that they seemed to pile up on each other. "But...there's trouble at the studio" Now her voice grew quickly serious.

"Oh?" He could only guess, and strangely enough didn't care.

"Karla didn't show up on the set yesterday."

"I didn't think she would. Anything else new?"

She gave him a sharp look. "I guessed something was wrong, Joe, when you called me out of the blue like that and...asking me to drive out here to Tarzana—just like that. What's wrong?"

He shrugged. "Everything. I blew it with Karla, I think. And she's blowing it with the studio."

114

"Isn't there anything you can do about it?" She sounded honestly concerned and he turned to look into her face. How lovely and tender, understanding and sweet she seemed. Suddenly he wanted to tell her everything, right down to the dirtiest detail; but that was impossible. Yet, strangely enough, even though he hardly knew Carol Fenton, he felt it was possible to talk to her as he might his closest friend.

"I could go back to Karla, get on my hands and knees and beg—that might work," he announced bitterly.

"What happened?"

"I just couldn't take it." He shrugged again. Offered her a cigarette, took one for himself, and lighted them. "It's all complicated...and I don't know if you'd understand."

"Maybe I can guess?" she offered carefully, not looking at him.

"I doubt it."

"It's strange, isn't it? Me being here. I really shouldn't considered what...well, what's between you and Karla. She sounded a little bitter, even angry."

"It's not the way you think, Carol." He spoke the words so softly that at first it was difficult to tell if she heard them.

"You *are* having an affair with Karla, aren't you?" There was a sharp edge to her voice.

"Not an affair," he corrected, beginning to warm up to the conversation. "Not what I call an affair, anyway!" It was obvious that Carol realized what was happening—or at least in part. The relationship between the two of them was rather strange, especially considering the fact she was also working for the woman.

"I don't know what you think of me, Carol," he continued, "but nothing in life is very simple—so I'm learning."

"You really don't have to explain, you hardly owe me an explanation. After all, we *aren't* lovers."

The last had popped out so quick that it left both of them startled.

Joe realized that he felt like a lover to Carol. In a very special sway. He felt as if they had known one another for a very long time; that they could talk pretty honestly about things. And most of all, he really wanted to make love to her. It was an alarming realization, since they had only been out

115

twice, once by accident the other a planned date and only kissed one time. Only once?

Emotion waved through him, so strong it was hard to keep it out of his voice.

"Carol, try to understand...no—just listen for a moment and I'll somehow get it out." He took a drag of the cigarette, then finished off the martini. "Karla is business—totally. Ugly business, if you want the truth! I don't know if you realize exactly what kind of woman she really is. I'm not quite sure, myself. But this has all happened against my will. Can you believe that?"

She turned, stared at him for a moment. "Not really."

When he didn't say anything to that, Carol stated: "You are supposed to be a man. Surely a woman like Karla can't dictate to you. Nobody can make you do something which is totally against your will—without holding a gun at your head. Karla doesn't have any gun at your head—or does she?"

"Not the kind you mean. She holds a contract over the agency's head."

"You mean she's blackmailing you? That hardly sounds reasonable. Really, Joe, do you expect me to believe that?" She suddenly stood. "I don't know why I came here—but it's getting us nowhere."

Without a word, Carol suddenly started out of the cocktail lounge.

Joe rushed after her, caught Carol's arm as she was stepping onto the sidewalk.

"Please!" he pleaded, desperately.

Forcing her to face him, he was startled to see tears streaming down her cheeks.

"Carol. I'm sorry. What'd I do?" But he knew what had caused this reaction; or was pretty sure.

"Carol, promise me you'll wait...I have to pay the check." She merely stared up at him, eyes pleading. "Carol please, promise me."

After a moment's hesitation she nodded.

Once he had paid the check, he returned to Carol, who had by now gained control of her emotions.

"That was silly of me, really." Her voice was high, a lit-

116

tle forced.

"Carol, I didn't call you to talk about...Karla." He took her arm, heading toward where he parked his car.

"I know," was her simple answer.

"I just wanted to see you. I had to talk to somebody."

She laughed. "That's flattering."

"No...I didn't mean it that way. It's just that … well for the last three days I've been thinking things over—about my life—and about you. Especially you, Carol. You kept popping up at the oddest moments." He helped her into his car and then rushed around to the driver's seat. Once sitting behind the wheel, he cried: "What about your car?"

Joe looked doubtful.

"I took a cab. Let it go at that?" Her voice was so sharp that it startled Joe to silence.

He started the car and headed east on Ventura, towards Hollywood. They rode in silence for a long time, and not until they had passed Sherman Oaks did he find the words to start the conversation again.

"When I get out of this immediate jam, Carol...I want to see you...see you a lot. Do you understand what I'm talking about?"

"Yes," she said in a small voice.

"I mean it."

"I guess you do believe that."

"Now what's that mean?" He stopped for a red light and turned to study her features.

"Just that this isn't the time to be talking about...well... you are involved with Karla—and until you can untie that knot, don't you think it would be better if we didn't see each other anymore? I mean, like this?" Her gaze was so level, the expression on her face so bland that it was impossible to fully understand exactly what she was saying.

"It's not that simple, Carol." His voice was almost pleading.

"Then why don't we just make it simple? As it stands right now, you might do terrible damage to your father's business—and you *are,* like it or not, Karla's present lover." The last was snapped out in total bitterness. "It was a mistake my coming to you like...well, *will* you take me home, please?"

Without another word, Joe started the car. His own mind was in a whirl of confusing thoughts. The only thing that counted was the fact he wanted Carol very much. Nothing else mattered, and no matter what it cost him, he would see to it that Karla knew he meant business this time.

Chapter Fifteen

"For God's sake," Mr. Blake cried, fairly pounding his desk in anger, "grow up, Joe!"

"Surely you aren't serious," Joe Blake countered, still fighting a terrible hangover. He'd just announced that he would have nothing more to do with Karla Kane. The look of disgust and determination on the older man's face startled Joe.

"I'm damned serious. I don't give one damn what you do afterwards. As far as I'm concerned, you've become a wash-out. I thought you had more guts than that. The first problem and you come crying to poppa. Well, just get this through your blasted head: there's no crying to poppa. You're a grown man, or are supposed to be. To say the least, I'm highly disappointed in you, Joe."

With that the old man sat back in his swivel chair. "You've not only caused a lot of trouble with the studio for us—but Karla is furious. And I can't say I blame her. She told me the whole story over the phone from Ventura, Monday morning. What kind of a bastard are you?"

Sick, his head throbbing, mouth dry, Joe held back the urge to shout. He managed to keep his voice level and soft.

"I don't know what she told you, but you can believe me there was no other way."

"Son, in the first place, a gentleman doesn't leave a lady in a hotel—taking the only car! How can you rationalize that?" The man's voice was cold, eyes deeply tired.

"One: Karla isn't a lady by any interpretation of the word. She's a tramp, slut—a damned demanding bitch who uses men as slaves, not lovers. You don't know what went on in that hotel room."

"I can imagine. And I don't care. I don't care what you *think* she is. It doesn't matter if she's all the things you said and more—but she's above all a female—and more important, the top account this agency has." Again his father stood. "I've worked hard to build this business, and nobody, not even my own son—for whom I did it all—is going to blow it away. And certainly not over some hot cunt that is demanding his services as a stud. You go over there and screw the woman silly, until she screams uncle or whatever she does when happy and content. I don't care what you have to do to please her. That's your job. Like it or not! The lady has rights! And I grand them fully to her! Got that?"

"Crap!"

"Women have rights. You treat them proper and they'll melt into your arms and do anything you expect. Karla just wants to be loved. Love the crap out of her! She's just a poor little female...have a heart! About time you learned how to treat a lady.

"Don't give me that, dad. I've seen the way you've worked this business. And you have no bloody respect for women! Damn you! I've seen the way you were with mother—the nights, endless ones, when she had to be alone. And I wouldn't be surprised if you'd been sleeping out on her like you have been on this present Mrs. Blake!"

His father moved around the desk so fast that it was impossible to react before the older man slapped a hard hand across Joe's face. "Don't you ever make moral judgments about me or your mother. What went on—or didn't go on—between the two of us is none of your business. You will never speak of that matter again to me. Do you understand?"

Joe's silence answered him.

"Now," his father stated matter-of-factly, moving back to his chair, "you will go to Karla Kane and you will get down on your hands and knees and beg, if that's necessary. You will make things good between the two of you until that picture is finished and we can sign her to a contract. Do *you understand?*"

"And if I refuse?"

"You won't refuse because you have a responsibility to yourself and to me. You got us into this jam, and you will get us out of it. You will handle Karla Kane until she signs up with us again, and you will continue to do so until she gets tired of you—which ever comes first. And you will make sure that the break-off is on high friendly terms." His eyes glared at Joe like some stranger staring at a creature he disliked.

"You don't want to hear my side of the story?" Joe managed, stunned by the other's statements.

"I don't care about your side of the story. It will not bring in any money." Throwing his hands up into the air, Mr. Blake cried: "What's wrong with you? This is Karla Kane! A sex symbol. A woman every man in America—all across the western world—would give anything to possess. I'm not asking you to take poison. I'm merely asking that you play ball with this until it's over. Ball her left and right, and down the middle. Lick her like a candy bar! Neither of us asked for it to happen like this, but we're in it and we have to do the best we can. That's life. That's what it is all about. You start something and you do the best you can to finish it—and on top. I won't even mind if you fail, just so long as you try."

"Until I die?" Joe inquired bitterly.

Laughter mocked him. "How you kids can dramatize things. She's not going to kill you. She's only a woman. So she likes to control a relationship between a man and herself. There are a lot of women like that. After all, Karla Kane has been a star for a long time. You have to understand that she is getting to the age when youth is slipping away. Her own insecurity is probably driving the poor woman out of her mind. Plus—who knows, maybe she's going through the change of life a little early! Have some manly consideration for her, Joe. Any way you look at it, Karla Kane is a woman—a female.

"Treat her like you cared—maybe things will just work themselves out naturally."

His father stood, moved around the desk again. As Joe stood to leave, a heavy arm was thrown about his shoulders. "She's spoiled. That's part of it. Pamper her for a few more weeks—things will probably simmer down. Then we'll both have good laugh over it."

Joe felt lost, then surrendered to the reality. He had

started things and had to finish them off. After that maybe he'd just quite this job. Until then, he had to complete what had been started. He owed the agency that much; if not his father, too.

As they reached the door Mr. Blake said: "Oh, yes, I almost forgot, there was a call from Larry Bershaw about a girl you turned over to him last week. Gloria...something. Seems she worked here. She quit this week. Well, the thing is, Larry assured me that she's star material. He wants us to arrange something for her. Why don't you handle it. I'm sure, since you've started the show, you might like to finish it. Pretty girl?"

He sighed, shrugged.

"Sexy, I guess," he admitted, with a weak smile. Suddenly even Gloria Davis seemed refreshing after Karla and what faced him in the coming weeks—probably months.

"Look, son," Mr. Blake said almost tenderly, with deep understanding in his voice, "believe me, nothing is forever. I know what I'm asking. I realize I was a little hard on you a few moments back, but I had to make you realize how important this thing is—and that...well, to be honest, I know Karla can be a pain—but if you put this over, believe me, you'll rate gold stars and it won't be long before I can retire and take that world tour I've been talking about for years. You've shown a lot of talent and the professionals in the business, like Harv Freeman, admires and respects you. You're not afraid to talk back to the big brass, and that's good, if you know how to do it. From what I've learned, you're going to be a top man—if you only grow up."

Then he added just before Joe turned to leave the office. "One piece of advice. Making Karla happy does not necessarily mean you have to be pushed around. What goes on between a man and woman is something which only the two involved know how to handle. One has to play it by ear. Just don't be a damned fool and forget that all women want to believe they are loveable. A woman like Karla Kane, more than others. She's had many unhappy love affairs. Her marriages were a flop. She realizes that it is probably her fault—but can't admit it to herself. So...if you just remember to be a gentleman—and a man. It takes more guts to face up to a

122

problem than walk out on it. Solve the problem, son. Don't turn away from it, because in the long run it will hurt *you* more than anybody else."

Joe felt a sudden pang of guilt, and didn't know why. His father has always had the talent of making people feel they were wrong, even if the opposite were true.

"Okay. I'll give it the old college try." He managed to throw his father a warm smile.

"That's not good enough. College boys don't know what the world's about. Give it the army try—no way out but success or total defeat."

STAR BITCH, BY CHARLES NUETZEL

Chapter Sixteen

"What's this between you and Carol Fenton?" was Karla's first statement after letting Joe into the house. It was so startlingly unexpected that he was unable to even speak.

"Come on into the den—fix yourself a drink," she invited sweetly, taking his hand, warmly squeezing the fingers.

This was the last thing he had expected. All the way from the office to Karla's house, he'd dreaded the scene which had to follow his appearance. Instead she'd merely opened the door, looked at him for a quick moment, then flashed a smile and asked the question about Carol.

What did she know? His mind screamed while sitting at the bar, legs shaking from the reaction.

When she handed over straight gin, her famous idea of a martini, Joe's hand felt like it was trembling. He gulped the gin down without any reaction.

"Well, Joe, I'm waiting for an answer," she stated, sitting next to him.

"I don't know what you're talking about," he announced carefully. "What's supposed to be between us? I've seen her a couple of times here— that's about it."

"You're a damned liar!" She spat savagely out. "A bastard and a liar. But we'll go into the bastard part later. Right now I want an answer to my first question and it better be good. I know more than you suspect."

"Oh? What's there to know?" Joe inquired, tensing for the obvious explosion about to take place. A grinding pain hit his stomach.

"Plenty. You've been seeing her on the side. Don't deny it. If you do...I warn you, love, hell will fall down on you." Her voice was so sweet that Joe almost cringed away from

125

her.

"What if I had seen her? You don't own me, Karla." He finished off the martini as if it were water.

"Want some more, sweet?" She poured more straight gin into the cocktail glass. "Drink up. I think you'll probably be needing it before long."

He simply stared at her unable to believe what was taking place. It was totally impossible to outguess Karla Kane.

"I'm waiting, love."

"There's really nothing to tell."

"*You son-of-a-bitch!* There's plenty to tell, and you know it. Harv told me plenty. Said you suggested her for that bit part. Said you warned her about not letting him play little games with her. Now, when and where did you do all this, sweet?" The sharp edge to her voice was accented by a fiery flare of vicious hate in her eyes.

"Oh, for God's sake, Karla, I don't know why you're making so much out of it. To be truthful I didn't put enough importance on the matter to make a report to you."

"But you lied just now about seeing her. So you are lying now, aren't you?" she demanded like a district attorney hammering away at a helpless witness.

"I bumped into her one day at the drug store. What the hell was I supposed to do, ignore her? It was lunch time and I...well offered to buy her lunch. It's as simple as that. We got to talking and she mentioned the fact that she was interested in acting...so when Harv said there was a part in your film, it was a natural."

"Obviously you wouldn't mind her having the part, so I suggested Miss Fenton."

"Miss Fenton? So formal?" she said cattily. "And all so innocent? Then why didn't you mention it in the beginning?"

He sighed, then told her, "Under the circumstances do you really think it would have been wise? I mean the present circumstances? I hardly think you'd have believed me if I'd told you the truth."

"What makes you think I believe you now?" she harped back. "I don't believe you. But it doesn't matter, does it?"

Without waiting for his answer, she stated: "In the first place, thou shalt not see Carol Fenton again, thou shalt not see any woman other then myself again—or she is out of the film, and you are out of a client—me! Understand, sweet love?"

"You certainly have it all mapped out, don't you?" he countered, bitterly, refusing to look at her.

"I have it worked out exactly as I want it. You don't have a leg to stand on, after what you did Saturday. That was a dirty trick, and I won't forget it, Joe."

Karla laughed harshly. "You know, sweet, you aren't the only stud in the world."

"Then why don't you find somebody else to play your little games?"

"Because right now I like you best." Then fixing herself another drink, Karla continued talking.

"You know that clerk at the hotel? Well, love, I wasn't about to be without a man."

"Don't be disgusting!" he spat out, grabbing the bottle of gin and refilling his glass.

"There's nothing disgusting about a little old fashioned sex party. And was he *fucking* surprised!" Her laugh was coarse and biting.

"I don't give a damn." He gulped on the gin.

"I do. And I want to tell you all about it."

"Forget it, Karla, I don't want to listen." He faced her to make the point more powerful.

"Little love, what you want and don't want doesn't make one crap of difference to me. You'll sit here and listen to what happened after you left me up in that hotel all alone. You will sit here and look at me and you will listen to each and every word I have to say. Do you quite understand, love?"

He started to turn away, and her hand reached out, clamped hard on his cheek, urging it back toward her. "You'll listen."

For a moment Joe was tempted to get up, leave, then realized that he did have a responsibility to the agency and his father and to himself to see this through, even on Karla's terms.

"Okay, I'll listen."

Karla nodded, satisfied. "Well, I told him to come up to

the room when he was off, with a bottle of whiskey. I don't know what he expected—but I imagine he was hoping. He didn't expect to find me lying on the bed, naked. The look on his face was fantastic. It was like some old silent movie. He almost dropped the bottle. I told him to open up the booze and have a drink.

"You know," she said, reaching for a cigarette, "he was fairly trembling. I could hardly keep from laughing. When I grabbed his arm a little later and put his hand on my breasts, I think he was about to fall apart. I told him he was good looking and I liked good looking guys and that I wanted him to make love to me. He fairly went purple with embarrassment. But when I started undressing him—like I do with you—he got greatly excited. I could see he was going to feel great, just the sight of...well, you know what I mean. He had a real man-size one, too! I'll tell you." Her eyes moved down to accent her words. "Believe me, for such an average guy, I wouldn't have thought...it almost frightened me in an exciting way."

She laughed again. "Boy, when he started on me, I thought it would never end. He couldn't get enough of kissing my breasts...then later he was all over me. Guess the unexpectedness of it all and, after all, what was he but a two bit hotel clerk, making love to one of the most glamorous female stars in motion pictures. The first one, though, was too fast. I think the whole thing just over-excited him. But later he got better. Real good. The last time—well past two in the morning—was great...real big blasting great. I thought he'd never stop...it drove me wild with pleasure over and over again."

"Why didn't you stay with him, then!" Joe snapped, sick at her story.

"Because, love, as great as he was, you're the best there is. And I want you—and I'm going to have you. I do hope you understand that totally." Her hand patted his cheek. "You are a real big lover in every way. It ain't what you got, but the way that you do it. And you got it, too. So...why should I take little old hotel clerks. Oh, for kicks, when my love has walked out on me, yes...that's something different, if you know what I mean. Then I'll take any stud that happens along. Now, I don't want that, love—and I don't expect you to ever do anything like you did to me again. You will be a good little boy, and you will slave to please me, do you quite know what I am talking about? I'm Mistress of the House, and you're my love slave...to be used and abused anyway she so decides. When I saw take it out, you'll unzip. If I say kiss me deep, down in the heart of Sexes! If I say lick it—"

"You've made your point quite clear. I'm all love and kisses at the Star Bitch's call!"

Suddenly Karla's slapped a hard hand across his right cheek, then her hand slapped back again. "You ever do that again and I'll kill you, I swear!"

Stunned, not daring to move or speak, Joe stared at her, controlling such violence that he had never felt in his life.

She slapped him again so hard that his ears rang. "You ever do it again ...you'll be sorry."

Suddenly Joe grabbed at Karla, his hands were at her throat, fingers squeezing violently to choke the life from her.

Then just as suddenly, partly because of the cold, confident look in Karla's eyes, he slowly released his hold.

"That wasn't very smart," Karla choked out some moments later. "It wasn't very smart at all, love. I'll make you pay plenty for it. You'll see just how demanding little Karla can really be."

She stood. "Under all this clothing is nothing but me. You *will* now, love, get down on your knees and you will start undressing my body and you will do things with your hands and lips which will be exciting to me and you will make it good or so help me, you'll wish to God you had."

Joe sat there on the barstool unable to believe her words. His hands were trembling with rage, his mind rebelled from even touching Karla Kane. It seemed fantastic that he'd gotten himself into such a mess.

For a moment he considered the thought of just turning around and walking out; then remembered that Karla could call off the part for Carol Fenton, could drop the agency and do even more damage to his father's business than that, if she really tried.

Then he remembered several things. Regardless, Karla

Kane had a good body. A man could react to a good, sexy body. She knew how to use that body, and she was an excellent love-mate. This was, after all, one of the top sex queens in Hollywood. Every man in the world desired the chance to possess her.

And what, really was she demanding? A sex party. How many times had he made those same demands, more subtly, to young girls. And it couldn't last for long with Karla—not forever. It would only seem that way.

"Well, love, you have been given your part to play, and you will do so immediately, because Karla is hot for you— and what Karla's hot for she gets. *Now!*"

Finishing off his drink, Joe slowly stood, moved to Karla, and forced himself to slip his arms around her waist. But when he attempted to draw her close, to kiss those sensual lips, she held back.

"I said, on your knees. And I meant just that, love. You will get on your knees before me, and you will beg forgiveness with your hands and with your lips and if your tongue speaks the right kind of language to my body as you undress me, I might decide to forgive you—and then you will have me being a nice little girl." Then almost as an afterthought, she added: "And don't forget there are a lot of men I've known and done favors for—men in high places with powerful connections with questionable parts of society. I don't think it is necessary to spell it out completely to you, love, so I'll just put it nicely. If you don't prove to be just as exciting as I know you to be, you might end up in the gutter one night with many bones broken and your ability to satisfy women fairly out of commission—for life."

Oddly enough, Joe didn't doubt her words in the least, and what was more terrible he realized she could probably get away with it,

Slowly, Joe started to slip down onto his knees. Oddly enough there was a strange, pervert instant thrill at what they were doing. The play was real, the act intense, and her demands serious—yet there was much to it that rang nothing more than wildly erotic fantasy. And that element raged real excitement through him. Meeting her demands would hardly be without its rewards. He was already fully aroused.

130

His bands reached out for Karla's hips, drew them close, his fingers reached up and pulled the zipper at the back of her dress.

"That's right, love," she said sweetly, caressing his neck with tender fingers. "You got me excited already. I think our arrangement is going to be far better from now on. I believe you are going to be…oh, honey, that's good, I like it when your lips do things like that. You do know how to please little Karla, don't you." She trembled, then clawed at his neck as the dress fell to the floor.

As Karla had stated, there was nothing on under the dress, and her Goddess body stood towering above him, lustfully awaiting the love slave's servicing to its needs. The very sight of her made him almost wild with lust, he wanted to ravish her.

"Now, love, start really exciting me. I want the best first—I demand your lips to kiss me until all the fires are screaming, until every nerve has burned to raging pain, until I'm insane and out of my mind for the final act. Then you'll give the best show you've ever given a girl in your life. You do understand? Only then do I want to feel you climbing into me, so deep that I almost choke on your delicious…cocktail deluxe! Understand baby, my babe, my lovin' little boy with the big one getting all burned up and ready for me. Make me ready for it. Make me burn. Make me shiver all over. Oh, yes…smother your lovely lips against my flesh until I scream for mercy!"

If the raging fire hadn't been lighted, like a switch being snapped into place, the whole scene would have seemed hysterically perverse, almost grotesquely disgusting. But there was nothing gross or ugly about this woman's body. She was a heavenly goddess of physical perfection, totally offering itself to him to feast upon like a starving man. And she made his body scream for a total banquet of her flesh. It was impossible not to fully respond, without any resistance. She wanted him to ravish her and that's exactly what would happen, until they were both beyond moving.

Her hands drew him to her and there was nothing to do but prove exactly how much he did understand her meaning.

STAR BITCH, BY CHARLES NUETZEL

Chapter Seventeen

Gloria Davis sat in front of Harv Freeman, remembering everything which had been told to her about the man. This was important to her, and she did not plan on making any mistake. Harv would want to make her, right now, if possible. She didn't mind giving him a little, just so she got what she was after.

There were several weapons at her command, besides a luscious body.

His eyes were centered on her low-cut neckline, to the points of her breasts which strained against the tight sweater.

"Well, dear, I've been told by two very important men that you might be of some use to us here at the studio. As a favor to them, I'm giving up a lot of valuable time to see you. I do hope it will prove worth it." He was sitting in the large leather chair to her right; she had been positioned on the sofa, which probably made into a bed.

"I believe you will find the time well spent," she offered, smiling warmly. "But, naturally I do expect some assurance that no matter what happens between the two of us during this interview or later, that you do intend to give me a contract as Mr. Blake said you would. Larry Bershaw told me to remind you he has never led you wrong—and that he promises that any investment you might make in my future will be backed by his reputation and teaching. Am I correct in assuming that you respect the man's opinion?"

For a moment Harv Freeman stared at her, then a slow smile sprayed across his lips. "You do have a way of coming to the point, don't you?"

"Well, Harv, you don't mind my calling you that, do you?" Without waiting for him to answer, she continued. "I think you're a darling man. And what I've been told about you, there isn't a thing you won't do for people who *really* cooperate totally. Isn't that right?" Her words were patterned after the material Larry Bershaw had given her. The instructions had been complete—backed by Joe Blake's promise that a contract would be in the offering, assuming she played her cards right with Freeman.

"I've been known to be very generous to people who are open and honest to me. Now, even then, I do expect some returns for any investment. If you can't act—though I'm assuming you can because of what Larry told me—there will be other means of making a profit with you."

"I understand, Harv. Larry told me all about the promotion trips you send young starlets on—and some of the little favors they give out to the right men. Isn't that what you were talking about? Bodily favors?"

He nodded, still staring at her breasts.

Gloria Davis felt a complete sense of power. Things had been happening fairly fast, but not illogically. Her date with Joe Blake that evening had paid off in great profits. Her affair with Larry Bershaw had become quite seriously involved. The man had taken a personal liking to her, especially because there were so few girls willing to go in for his kind of kicks; at least with the same kind of wild freedom she displayed. She liked sex; and it showed when she climbed into bed with a man.

Larry had said this was very important when used as a weapon. *"Never let a man use you—your body is the only thing you really have to sell, so make sure they pay the right price and know that is what they are going to have to pay!"* he'd told her. But more important he'd said that it wasn't always necessary to sleep with a man to get ahead, that there was a lot of Hollywood brass who wouldn't sleep with a woman even with a gun at their heads. They were looking for talent to promote and nothing more. But Harv Freeman was something different. In some cases he would help a girl out without sleeping with her; but to make sure, to really put on the screws, it was far better to play the game his way.

"I'm willing to take directions and do anything I can to help out my employers. I believe it is very important to make a good impression on anybody who might help the studio. Don't you think that's true?"

"It certainly is."

"Well, now, Harv, I realize you have not seen me do any reading, but you have seen me...and I believe that you believe Larry when he says I can act. Is there anything else you require before saying one way or another what you might be able to do for me?" Her phrasing had been carefully worked out between Larry and herself. This was the pay off, the moment when he would make his first move to climb into bed with her—and the moment when she would make her final verbal play.

"If I get your meaning, sweetheart, you're offering to let me make a total study of what you have to offer. And I do believe you expect me to fully enjoy it, from beginning to end."

"I'm certain you will," she promised, smiling generously at him.

"But I smell a Bershaw trap in your wording."

Gloria laughed brightly, then winked. "It is rather a long way to say: if you want to sign me to a contract, and can provide strong enough evidence to that fact, then I'll be more than willing to let you make a full study of what you are buying. To see it, feel it, experience it in total detail, for a prolonged afternoon. I'm, after all, here to please you...and I'm free for the rest of the day. I was told to clear my slate in order to do your bidding."

It sure was a corny script, but rather funny and fun to play out. She was actually enjoying herself.

"And, what if I don't like what I've bought?" Freeman countered, a twinkle in his eyes.

"Oh, come on, Harv, you can't really sit there and eye my body like you have, knowing what Larry told you about me over the phone yesterday—and knowing Larry is not the kind of guy to give the wrong facts to important men like you—and say you won't like what you're buying."

"You *are* blunt." He grinned, pleased by her boldness.

"Let's be brutally honest," she suggested, being careful to watch the expression on his face. If there was any sign of irritation she'd have to back off. "This is really cut and dry, and we both know it. All the arrangements were made in advance. Mr. Blake has talked to you in private and come out with assurances that there's no reason in the world not to give a willing girl a break if she has the right material for the use you have in mind. In blunt terms, if I can't act, or can't cut the ice on film, you'll put me on your party girl list. That's the way you stated it to Joe Blake, isn't it?" Without waiting for an answer she quickly added: "And Larry has assured you that any efforts expended on my behalf will be will rewarded. You've seen half of the product, nicely wrapped up to tease you into wanting to unwrap it. So now I see no reason not to show you the rest."

With that, Gloria stood, reached around her back and unzipped the dress. The cloth fell in a ring about her feet. Immediately her bra slipped off large breasts which stood up proud and firm on her chest. Then she removed the rest of her clothing and stood before him in brazen invitation. "This is what you will be pleased to know is a woman who has nothing against an adult relationship between herself and a man. But I'm not about to be used and kicked aside. Why don't you call up your secretary and make arrangements for Mr. Blake's office to sign a contract with you for me."

It was some moments before Harv Freeman found his voice. "Damned, if you don't take it all!" he exploded. "What the hell makes you think you can tell me what to do? Where the hell did you get the idea that just because I see you naked I'll jump through rings? What kind of crap are you handing me?"

His face was a mixture of animal lust and raging anger.

Gloria just stood there before him, hands on hips, breasts thrust out, a smile playing on her lips.

"I'm really not telling you to do anything, Harv. Just that I know what you want—you know what I want. Can't we make a logical business arrangement about it, without playing coy?" She moved close to the desk, leaned across. "You would like to make love to me, wouldn't you?"

He gulped, then cried: "You little tramp, there're hundreds of girls willing to make love to me, and they are too stupid to realize it won't do them a damned bit of good. What do I have to have you for?"

136

"You don't. Do you?" She turned, leaned over and started picking up her bra and panties. Inwardly she was smiling to herself; things had developed almost exactly as she'd been told they would. Men like this were all too obvious. "Since you aren't interested, I guess there's nothing to do but leave."

"Hey, just wait a minute." His voice was husky, a low rasp.

"What for?" Gloria inquired, placing her bra over her breasts. She faced him, a sweet, innocent smile on her lips.

"You know damned well what for," he exploded, a sharp gleam to his eyes. "I've had every approach imagined to man—but this one is totally new. Who the hell told you what to do and say?"

"Larry Bershaw," she announced honestly with a grim smile. "Don't you think it was cute? Well, I mean, aren't I cute?"

She started to clip her bra into place and then slipped her panties on. "Larry said that the bold, shock approach would please you."

"What the hell are you doing?" he cried, alarmed, standing, reaching out a hand in her direction. "Don't get dressed, dear."

"Why shouldn't I? You saw what kind of body I have. Surely you don't want anything more? I just wanted to be sure you realized there wasn't one thing false about me. I wanted to be sure you knew just how desirable I was, and what kind of image I could project on the screen. After all, women like Karla Kane can't last forever and its just about time a new queen took over, don't you think? I'm only twenty-one—and there are a lot of years ahead of me before age starts showing on my body. Don't you think that's true?"

He started to say something, then moved around his desk. "Now, young lady, don't take me for a fool. I knew exactly what you were doing—and you realize that. You get out of those damned things, lay over there on the sofa and I'll join you for a real demonstration of your talents."

"What in the world for? You can get countless of women, who aren't smart enough to know that sleeping with you won't make a damned bit of difference. You said that yourself. Now, tell me, give me one good reason, why I should allow you any special considerations? Surely a big, important man like you can think of something," she suggested with a wicked wink.

He laughed, then backed away. "Since you know it wouldn't do you any good, why would you?"

"Because, I think it might be fun, once we have gotten all the arrangements in order," she offered with another flashing, inviting smile. "We could have oh so much fun together. I just know it!"

He moved to his desk, mumbling to himself, "I've never seen such a thing...in all my years in this blasted business...this woman takes all the awards for brazen, bold, unexpected brassiness. Blast you, woman!" He looked up across his desk at her. His eyes went wide, because Gloria had slipped out of her bra and panties and was laying on the couch, waiting for him, "Blasted woman!" he cursed, picking up the intercom and then saying:

"Call Joe Blake and tell him I think—" then looking at Gloria he changed that to, "I know we can make great use of the young lady he sent over this afternoon. We'll have a contract—yes, the standard six-month with options—ready for him and her to sign. Yes, get out a form and make it ready for us. But don't bother me for a little while. Okay? We have some very serious interviewing to do!"

Then he started toward Gloria a look of intense excitement in his eyes.

"You won't be sorry, Harv," she announced as he come to a stop over her. "I think we're going to have one wonderful relationship. I believe in making the guys who help me very, very happy. I mean to make you so very, very happy that you'll always remember this afternoon as one special ... loving time."

Chapter Eighteen

Carol Fenton was sitting on the lounge chair in the patio when Joe Blake stepped out from Karla's bedroom, a morning robe tightly drawn about his frame.

He looked at the young woman as he moved to the outdoor bar and poured himself a drink. A dim hangover was touching his head, and he needed to wash it away.

"Hi," he greeted, good-naturedly. "Surprised seeing you here."

She glanced at him, started to pull a towel over her bikini, to hide her lush, voluptuous body. "I didn't know you were here."

"What'd you expect?" He was still drunk from the drinks which had kept him going throughout the night with Karla. "Our queen has made her commands and the servants must obey."

Carol glanced toward the bedroom door. "Where is she?"

"Taking a shower, I would imagine. That's what she told me, anyway." He lifted the glass of straight gin to his lips and sipped. "How's the film coming?"

Carol refused to look in his direction. "Fine, I guess." There was a coldness to her voice.

Joe felt a momentary pang, then washed it down with the raw gin. For weeks now he had played the role Karla had demanded. This was the first time, though, that he'd met Carol Fenton at the house after having spent the night with Karla. It unnerved him, but the liquor haze and his own emotional mental block, which had turned him into a thing which merely existed, walled away almost all feelings.

"How can you do it?" Carol inquired in a soft voice.

139

"Do what?" He refilled the glass.

"You know exactly what I mean." Her eyes flashed toward his, then returned to the pool to gaze blindly there.

"There are some things people must do, regardless." He moved toward Carol, stood over her, only a yard away.

How desirable she looked. The swell of her breasts against the narrow band of the top of the bikini excited him. He looked away at the pool. Guilt flushed raw at his emotions. How could he stand here and talk to Carol—or even face her? Karla had driven him that far down the road of destruction; to the point where he didn't even make sense any more. Life had become a series of momentary actions bent on surviving another hour longer. Each day had become a nightmare of existing. It had to end, someday. And until then he was totally turned off and completely surrendered to Karla's lustful desires and body. Under some circumstances it might have seemed an ideal trap. To him it was a necessity to keep things going. As long as he didn't have to deal with his feelings.

And Carol made him want to run as fast as possible, away. He wanted to take her hand and drag her bodily after with—to some safe place where they could make love. He wanted to be in her arms, to find reality there.

"I have to see you, Carol," he whispered.

"No, that's impossible."

"I have to. I'm going out of my mind." He laughed slightly. "That's very funny. Insane, really!"

"You going out of your mind?" Carol inquired in a cold voice. "Oh, come on!"

"No—laugh as if we're just joking—casually. If Karla guesses what I'm really saying. .

Carol forced a laugh, then whispered: "You can hardly be serious."

"I'm very serious, Carol." Choked emotion caught in his throat. For three weeks he'd been playing total slave to a bitchy, perverse woman who called herself a human being. Several times he'd come close to the point of killing Karla. "I have to talk to you, please."

There was a short silence, then Carol said: "Okay. When and where?"

140

"Your place —"

"No."

"Your place—or a motel—I don't care," she countered a little harshly.

"My place." He thought quickly, then when Karla's voice called from the bedroom, he said: "Eight, tonight. I'll get away from her, somehow."

"Joe—please!" Karla cried.

"Okay, coming."

When he had entered the bedroom, Karla glared at him. "What were the two of you whispering about?"

"Nothing."

"Tell me, Joe, or I'm warning you..." Her eyes flared with sudden emotion.

"I was arranging to meet her tonight. Some private motel where we could screw our brains out! Right? How do you like that?"

Her biting laughter mocked him. "I can just imagine that. You wouldn't dare do that. You aren't that desperate yet. Not by a long run." She patted his cheek. "Though I can image you desiring the little prude. But good luck. She ain't givin' out to no man or woman!"

"So...you see, I tell you the truth and you don't believe me—so why invent a lie?" He grinned sheepishly, automatically kissed her lips, as she expected him to. He had learned in these last days how to fake real feelings as an actor much on the screen. He played out his lines as if under the direction of a great director. He had to. She was too smart to be easily fooled.

Her house robe was the only thing she wore, and Joe dutifully slipped his hand under the folds and touched a well formed warm breast. He teased the nipple, squeezed it between thumb and fingers.

"You beast! You sure know how to make me hot." She laughed coarsely, a sound which rang loud. "Why not do it now?"

"Anything you demand, Karla. You know that. I simply can't get enough of you!"

She parted the robe and displayed her naked form to him. "You are well trained, love."

"You trained me." The words came automatically without any thought. He had been living this way for days, sort of moving through life like a dazed robot, without feelings, without any sense of reality—except for a few sober moments when reality rushed in with crushing force to create such hatred it was almost impossible to control. Having a quick drink, followed by another, had soothed the rage away. Now he drank mornings and all through the day until night. Slow, even drinking that kept him just slightly tilted from reality; not drunk, but not completely sober. It was the only way to suffer through the times with Karla.

Karla lay down on the bed, spreading the robe away. "Come, love, before we have to split. I do have an appointment this afternoon at the studios for a quick retake."

"You're going to be away?" he cried, as if in alarm.

"I told you. It might last into the late evening."

"Oh, what the hell can I do to keep entertained?"

"Go to some motel with that prude little shit Carol and ravish her. If she'll let you!" she laughed mockingly.

"Maybe I'll do just that!" he threatened with an evil mock-grin.

"Good luck, hon! You'll be bored to death! That I can promise you! Unless you like deflowering young chilled virgins!"

"Hardly my type of fun time. Never could understand guy who wanted to have virgins!"

"A power play, honey. And I think those men are afraid to face a real woman like me. A virgin has nothing to compare her first love to, so how does she know he's a washout?" Her laughter was cruel, cutting. Then softening slightly, she said; "If you want that kind of action, you're welcomed to it, hon. But right now…you have me and when I'm done with you you'll be too pooped to…well, pop!"

"So far you haven't managed to do that," he noted with some perverse pleasure. The woman was sadistic.

"Well, we can try. I was told me to relax this morning—so you relax me. Okay? Give me something to blow my mind! I need a bit of relaxation messages, all over, deep and penetrating. You know exactly what I need, baby!"

Joe pulled off his morning robe, knowing what was expected.

Karla laughed. "Joe you are wonderful!" Her voice was loud enough to carry out onto the patio.

"Not so loud."

"You afraid little Miss Prude will hear? Carol," she called, "you better go on home. I won't be needing you for the rest of the day. A woman likes some privacy with her lover."

"Shut up." Joe spat out the words like a snake striking its victim.

"Why? Are you afraid she might guess what we are about to do?" Karla mocked him with a sweet grin. "We *might* shock her at that. After all, she is such a prude. Probably thinks we are playing cards or something." Changing the conversation in one quick moment, as was her habit, Karla commanded: "Come over here and kiss my titties. They're getting tingly just thinking about it. I want your lips to fold around them, to feast on them, and I want you to thrill them and I want your body to move to mine and I want all the good things it can give little Karla Kane. Explode your male body all over me!"

As he moved to her, all the time forcing himself not to think about the terrible hatred cutting through him, she blew up a kiss.

"Push-pull, click-click, love. That's what I want from you. Automatic lover who goes into action when little me tells him to." She cupped hands under her still breasts, pushing up their ripe pink nipples, waiting for his lips and tongue.

There was nothing to do other than as commanded.

As his lips folded around one quickly responding nipple, Joe fought down the desire to bite so hard that blood would flow.

"That's good, love. The other one, too. Don't let my other breast get...oh, yes. Do that again!"

He moved from one hardened nipple to the other until she was gently writhing under the kisses. Her hands went to his head, directed him back and forth, faster and faster.

Then he caressed her stomach and thighs, hard and quickly, the way she liked it, even clawing at the flesh.

Joe's thoughts shifted to Carol and the bikini which had

hardly done anything to hide her body. He would give almost anything to be with Carol. Immediately a sharp reaction jolted him at the thought. He tried to imagine this was Carol Fenton that he was about to posses, not Karla Kane.

"You are getting exciting," Karla almost sobbed. Then her hand made an exploration of his form until it had intimately learned the extent of his own excitement. "You are hot."

Without thinking, Joe started to slip across Karla's body, then positioned himself for the final lunge into her.

"No, wait. Please. I want to do something different." She started to turn around on her stomach, but Joe stopped her. "Do it animal style!" she pleaded.

"Shut up," he cursed, grabbing her shoulders and slamming her back against the bed.

"Joe—I gave you a command." Her eyes glared up at him. "You've cooled it."

His right hand suddenly slapped at her face and he fought the rushing urge to hit her with a doubled up fist until her features were nothing but a bloody mess. Instead his body rammed down hard, with amazing skill uniting with her. But the pleasure was brought on by the mental image of Carol Fenton. He kept his mind paralyzed by her vision, the full ripe breasts, the rounded hips, narrow waist, the voluptuous thighs and lovely sensual face. Carol was so different from Karla Kane. It was amazing what her mental image did to his body. He responded to her image, her phantom memory—but it was Karla's body that whipped violently against him, pinned to the bed like a bug. She gasped again and again, overwhelmed by his skilled love-making. For this time he was imagining being with Carol, loving her, and with every penetration his whole body was being passionately tender, stroking her with so much feeling that tearing screaming down his eyes at the wonder of it.

Karla's hands clawed at Joe, cutting the flesh at his back as sobs of joy and pleasure shook her lips and throat.

He only vaguely saw Karla's form under his, then he closed is eyes on reality and attempted to believe it was Carol Fenton.

The movement of his body slowed, became an even,

144

careful, loving rhythm. Every nerve wanted this to last, to be good and long, to take in every sensation as if it were some jewel that might shatter if approached too violently.

The body under his started going wild and at last there was nothing to do but play out the game Karla's way. By then, Joe didn't care much about anything. His own nerves were fired, flaring with anguished pain and pleasure. The final moments were like rockets exploding his head apart. Teeth clamped so tight they hurt, he orbited into outer space and then came crashing through the atmosphere, too exhausted to do anything other than fall down upon the soft cushion of the feminine form below him.

How long he lay there, Joe didn't know. Finally he came back to reality and lifted up from Karla Kane.

Standing, he felt a convulsive disgust at what had happened. If Karla guessed whose image he'd really been making love to, the bright happy light in her eyes would dull to insane rage.

She was beaming up at him, arms extended. "Oh, that was great. Just great, love. The best. The best there ever was. I thought you'd never stop. I never knew it could be so good that way...oh it was so good and loving and tender...I want more and more. You will do it again? Please, for me, for little Karla. Again...because I can't stand not having you do it again...you got to."

"For God's sake, have a heart." He fought down the desire to tell her to go to hell.

"Push-pull, click-clock, love. Remember. You move when I command." Her voice was hard.

Joe suddenly felt something snap inside him. It was difficult to tell exactly what caused the quick change. Probably, he realized with a flash, the fact that Carol had been out on the patio. It had been possible to play out the charade, knowing it would end in time, as long as Carol could be forgotten. But to have mentally been making love to Carol...

He knew it was impossible to continue with Karla. No matter what it might cost. It was just impossible.

Karla looked wantonly at him, licked her lips, and then rang trembling hands along her thighs. "I want it the other way, now. Animal style, Joe. You do know what I want. I'll be your little doggie!"

He stood there rigidly looking at Karla and all at once
nothing mattered much. Three weeks of this woman was six
too many for any normal man. He was becoming a drunk
because of her. With a quick realization he knew it wasn't
worth it; nothing was worth what he had to go through for
her.

"Come on, Joe, give it to me fast and hard. Be my great
big ape. My nice little doggie. I feel dirty, now. I want it real
dirty, Joe. Real mean and dirty."

He merely glared at her.

"What's wrong, love?" Karla inquired, totally ignorant
of the raging storm which had taken control of him.

"What kind of bitch are you? Surely you realize what's
going on—what's really going on. A woman like you—
desired by so many guys—doesn't need to do this. You don't
need me anymore than you need a whole in your head. You
act like some whorish queen slut making commands of a
slave." His words blurted out so coldly controlled, so evenly
that they seemed to take several moments for Karla to realize
exactly what he'd said.

"Love, surely you can't mean that," she warned.

"I don't know about you, Karla—and I don't give a shit,
any more. I can't take this any more. I *have* reached a point
where...oh, hell. Go to hell!"

Whipping around, Joe started out of the room.

"Don't move, Joe. Don't be a bloody fool. I warn you!"
she shouted.

"You just shove your warnings," he cried back, starting
to move the door open.

"You leave this room and I'll just put in a call to some
friends of mine—remember what I told you?" Karla was
standing now, totally naked.

He turned and faced the woman. "Karla, what kind of
damned kicks are you getting out of this? You must know I
hate your guts. You must know the only reason I've been
able to stand it up until now is because I've managed to keep
a little drunk all the time—and I've done it only because of
the agency. But surely you can't want this kind of relationship with a man. Any woman alive would want to be desired

and desirable—and you are that in a basic animalistic way. You are beautiful in body—if only you were the same in spirit." He felt cold, unemotional. The words came out with a total lack of expression. He merely stood there staring at her, speaking like a man talking to a wall.

"Do you want to know the truth, love?" Karla inquired in the same sweet voice which was so dangerous. "Well, I'll tell you. I had decided I loved you—then returned to the hotel room and found you'd left. That love turned into something else; something I didn't even realize I possessed. Nobody has ever done a thing like that to me before. Now if you want to know what kind of kicks I get—its because I know you hate me, and that I can still make you get excited. That's power—that's being real powerful when you make somebody who hates you get excited. Make them want you so badly that they'll submit to any degrading demand! You're my slave!"

"A slut would make me excited if she was as filthy as you." This time it spat out with emotion. "Just grow up. You're spoiled rotten. You've had too many good things. Why don't you start facing up to life—why don't you realize that don't have that many years left in the business. Younger women will always be there to take your place."

"Oh, really? Well, I have a lot of good years going for me. Don't kid yourself. And just else what do you think I am, love?" she inquired, gliding across the room toward him.

"An attractive lady scared witless because she's getting older every day—like everybody else. So what's so special about Karla Kane that she can't grow older? And sure, you do have a good life ahead of you, and you have a long career in front of you, if you only play it smart. Why do you need a guy like me? You could find somebody willing to share you. There are a lot of guys who go in for the kind of stuff you like. But not me. So what do you really profit by abusing me? What the damned hell are you really gaining?"

She stopped in front of him. Her hands went to her breasts, lifted them upwards. "You will now get on your hands and knees and kiss them. Do you hear? And maybe I'll forgive you. Just maybe if you are good enough."

This part they had played over and over in the past couple of weeks. And he was simply finished. No more. Nothing matter but getting away from this woman, this trap, the horrible nightmare.

Joe looked at her, sighed and then without a word turned around and walked out of the bedroom.

Chapter Nineteen

Carol Fenton smoked nervously as she sat in the car next to Joe Blake. All these weeks, knowing what was going on between Joe and Karla, had been a terrible torture. She'd watched as Joe slowly became more and more distant, retarded from reality.

Joe had said hardly anything since picking her up at the apartment.

As they pulled up to his place, he finally announced: "I don't know where to start, Carol"

"From the beginning?" she offered, turning to look him in the face. How she loved the damned fool. It had all slipped up on her suddenly like a blow. This morning, that pleading. She knew how much he needed her; it was obvious. If only he realized what a damned fool he was being. Yet, it was not difficult to understand the pressures and demands which made it impossible for him to break from Karla. After all she was a very important person in the Hollywood circles, and no doubt about it, the woman was using that power to force Joe to bend to her will.

"There's really no beginning, Carol. Just that...first of all, I broke it off with Karla, this morning."

"You're kidding?" Hope choked her voice with emotion. She'd been out on the patio and heard some of the things which went on in the bedroom before it was possible to rush out of there.

"I don't really know what's going to happen, Carol. I mean, about...well, everything. I've made myself scarce, since this morning. You're the first person I've seen. The thing is...well, I've been doing a lot of thinking and—the way things stand right now, I just can't expect to keep the

149

job at the agency. Dad will be rightfully furious. He doesn't really understand—or won't allow himself to—how that...woman can be. He'll think I'm a kid who just quit. Well, maybe that's right."

"Don't, Joe. You know that's not right. I don't know how you put up with it this long. I don't know how I can even sit here with you—knowing what she made you....maybe because I realize how she put on the screws. I don't know. Maybe its something else." But Carol knew exactly what. it was. She loved Joe, regardless of his imperfections. She'd felt something from the very beginning, and having seen what a bitchy woman could do to him had actually made her love Joe more. Now that he'd had the guts to pull out before it was too late it made that love grow.

Joe shook his head. "I've been a damned bloody fool. But...the thing is...the future is a little hazy. Maybe I'll go into something like real estate. That might be a good idea."

Carol nodded, seriously. "Dad might help you on that. I *know* he would! You'd get along famously, I'm sure."

Joe shrugged. "Well...it's a thought."

He faced her, his hands reached out, cupped gently about her shoulders. "Carol, I don't know how to say this...and I have no rights...but...I've never felt...like this before...I mean, about a woman. If only I could find the words."

"Don't you want to go up to your apartment?" Carol suggested boldly, surprised by her own words, for she was offering much more than mere conversation. For the first time in her life she wanted to give herself to a man. There would be no guilt feelings. It was *right,* under these circumstances; and that was that. How different it all seemed, now. So simple. With the right man.

"That's not what I'm talking about, Carol. I'm talking about...love. I do love you. How it happened so fast, I don't know."

"Maybe it's just desire," she suggested.

"I believe I'm old enough to know the difference. If it were just desire I'd take you up to my apartment and seduce you. That would be the end of it. But I suddenly want something more than that. I want to organize my life and I want a

150

future which will have a solid direction. I don't know what you want, Carol—but I'd do my damndest to give what ever you wanted. Do you think you could...?"

A hot flush covered Carol's face and she felt a warm glow. "I do believe you are asking me to marry you?"

Joe nodded like a little boy, his head bobbing up and down wildly.

Carol flung her arms around his neck. "Oh, you don't know how happy that makes me. I do love you ..."

"How the hell can you?" he murmured against her throat. Then their lips were meeting, soft and warm, bodies crushed tightly together in a warm embrace.

"Let's go up to your apartment," Carol suggested as she pulled away from him.

"It's not necessary," he countered a little huskily.

"Who says it's not necessary? I love you. You love me. We desire each other. For the first time in my life I really want a man to make love to me—but only one man—and that's you. Please...let's start this all out right. We don't know what the future holds for either of us. But I do know one thing that you are going to be very important to me. We can face anything together. I'll talk to my father tomorrow about getting you into real estate, if that's what you want." Carol realized that Joe's emotions might be lying to him; that he might only think he loved her. But that didn't matter. She loved him, and being the woman she was, wanted to do everything in her power to make the man she loved happy. If one didn't grab life, take a chance, they might as well lay down and die.

* * * * * * *

When they approached his apartment door, Joe heard the phone ringing. Fumbling with the key, he opened the door, then rushing automatically toward the phone on the small living room desk, he hesitated.

"Well, aren't you going to answer it?" Carol laughed, closing the door.

"I don't know if I should," Joe pointed out, then on impulse picked up the phone.

"Hello?" he said. Then the person on the other end hung up.

"Well, that's that. Wrong number," he announced, replacing the receiver and turning toward Carol, who had come up beside him.

Her arms slipped around his waist. "I do love you, Joe—when you're this way."

"Meaning?" he countered, feeling like himself for the first time in weeks—even months. Their lips were only inches apart and he savored the waiting before kissing her.

"Meaning that you aren't under *her* influence." Her arms tightened their grip about waist and her cheek pressed his.

"Do we have to talk about her?" he countered, dreading even the thought of the woman.

All this felt like the calm before a storm which might totally destroy him. He remembered Karla's threat to call some of her underworld buddies. That was enough to shake any man up. Karla seemed like the kind of girl who would stop at nothing to get revenge—even murder if it was possible to get away with it.

He shook away the thought, centered all attention on Carol.

How do you seduce a virgin? he wondered. It had been so long, and at that time he'd been such a kid, that this was a totally new, unnerving experience. Suddenly the idea seemed perverse.

Carol, as if sensing his hesitation, moved her lips to his, parted and moist.

The offering was too sweet and innocent to ignore. As he felt her tongue move past his teeth, a thrill waved up through him. The softness of Carol's body, the way it clung to his was so wonderful and heady that control began immediately slipping.

How un-virginal her body was. Voluptuous: a woman greatly to be desired.

"Carol," he breathed, a moment later as they broke the kiss, "you don't have to…"

Her hand reached up and touched his lips. "Silence, my dear sweet love." Her voice was low and musical.

Taking his hand in hers, Carol pulled him toward the

152

door which obviously led to a bedroom. As if she had been in his apartment before, she skillfully led the way.

Suddenly, Joe realized, Carol was the seducer. And with this awareness came the knowledge that all women were the seducers—not the men as it might appear. If a woman didn't want to submit to a man, there was hardly anything he could do about it, short of rape.

Carol turned, presenting her back to him.. "Unzip me, please, darling."

Tenderly he moved the long zipper down to the base of her back, and then slipped his hands under the dress, around to the full swells of youthful breasts. He felt the nipples go hard through the bra under his first caresses. A moan of delight sounded from Carol's lips. Then she somehow managed to turn in his arms, the dress tangling in his hands; than a moment later it fell to the floor. She was kissing his face and neck and lips with passionate lack of control as his fingers worked the bra clasp, fumbling at first, then freeing it. With a giggle, Carol slipped out of the bra.

"I feel drunk," she murmured happily. She stood in front of him, honestly submissive to his gaze. Yet he was sure this was the first time Carol had ever been this naked before a man. This kind of wonderful gift was totally astonishing. She was offering herself, her virginal self, to the man she loved, as a total gift of love.

"You're the most lovely woman I've ever seen," he announced huskily, feeling emotions which had not touched him in years. In fact, Joe realized, he had never felt this way about a woman before. Even with Clara Henderson, it had been merely desire, he now knew this fact a very real.

With Carol Fenton, he felt wave upon wave of protectiveness.

"Damn it all, let's go get married" he blurted out.

"That's not necessary—right now, is it?" she countered in a voice that revealed her own amazement at the words.

"It's never necessary except with somebody you love very much. I think I'd almost rather wait until after the wedding." Though Joe knew that was impossible under the immediate circumstances.

"Maybe you would, Joe, but I will *not* wait!" Determina-

153

tion lighted her eyes as she slipped soft, velvet arms about his neck and pressed her breasts tightly to his chest. "I've wondered what it would be like the first time, Joe. I've always wondered. But I never...never guessed it would be this way."

Unable to control himself longer, Joe kissed her with such violent tenseness that at first he didn't hear the pounding on the front door.

Carol sighed. "Who could that be?"

"Ignore them."

He lifted her into his arms and started for the bed. Laying her down, he gently kissed each breast, experiencing such pleasure that it made him dizzy. Then he started stripping off his jacket and shirt.

"JOE BLAKE!" came the sound of a woman's voice calling from outside the apartment.

Ignoring the call, Joe slipped down on the bed and kiss Carol's lips and then caressed her breasts, cupping them gently. How he loved her. It seemed fantastic that she could even look at him after having watched on the side-lines while he'd been used as a love slave by Karla Kane.

Yet love did strange things to people and usually wasn't very logical.

"Joe Blake, it's Gloria! This is important, please answer. I *know* you're in there," shouted the female voice from outside.

"Damn it," he cursed, staring down at Carol who smiled and shrugged.

"Maybe," she said, "you better get rid of your other girls right now. I do not want to share you ever...*ever!*"

"You won't, ever," he promised.

Regretfully, Joe stood and went into the living room, then opened the front door.

Gloria Davis rushed in, her face a study in tense emotions.

"Where've you been all day?" she exploded. "Lost—but I've found myself." Gloria looked at his naked chest, then glanced toward the bedroom door.

"Sorry, Joe," she murmured, "but I think this is important."

154

STAR BITCH, BY CHARLES NUETZEL

"Think nothing of it," he said, not able to hide the bitterness from his voice.

"I didn't mean to break up some session...but, something happened. Several things, in fact. I was in your father's office this morning on business. The studio did a screen test on me and Harv Freeman flipped and wants to make a big promotional on me and—but that's not what I came here to tell you. Everybody has been looking for you. I promised your father that if I found you I'd call him immediately."

"Can't this wait until later?"

"No," she announced. "Karla...well, he better tell you."

Shrugging, Joe went to the phone. "Home or office?"

"Hospital, Hollywood-West."

"What the hell happened?" he cried, suddenly worried. "Is he all right—"

"He's fine, under the circumstances. But...it's Karla Kane—she tried to kill herself."

STAR BITCH, BY CHARLES NUETZEL

.

Chapter Twenty

How simple, tragic, and horrible it all seemed. Joe stood outside the hospital room, Carol and Gloria at his side, Harv Freeman and his father in front.

His father said: "Look, Harv, give the girl a break. Apparently she's had a pretty terrible shock."

"What about the studio? We don't need this kind of thing. It will hold up production and—we have other interests that can be a lot more profitable. Karla's been screwing her career the way she's been acting...*this* tops it!" Harv looked at Gloria, grinned wolfishly, made a motion with his right hand, and the woman moved close. "This girl here is going to be number one in the near future. I don't need to fool around with temperamental aging stars who—"

"What the hell are you," Joe blurted out, angered to the point of disgust. That woman inside there almost died today. You're already attempting to kill her career. Well, why don't you think of some way to fix things up so that she won't be such a headache? I've learned to know Karla—and I'll admit I don't like a lot about her...but she is a woman and a human being. Maybe if you guys started treating her with respect, and try making things easier...maybe a little pampering on the set—treat her like the star she is and has been—hell, you've all made enough money from her films—so you can ride through a little production set-back."

Harv glared at Joe, then at his father. "Well, you do have a point. I'm sorry about that."

Joe's father turned to him, snapped: "You're to blame for all this. If it hadn't been for you stepping all over the poor woman—what right do you have to talk about—"

Carol's voice cut in, "I don't think, Mr. Blake, that you

have a leg to stand on. I don't think you know what she did to your son. So why don't you just be quiet?"

Mr. Blake glared at Carol, then snapped:

"You're in Karla's picture, aren't you? The new young girl—and you have a big mouth."

Joe said in a very quiet way, "Dad, I believe you had just better stop it right there. This is not the time or place to argue. It is not the time or place to tell you that I'm quitting the agency business."

Both Harv Freeman and Gloria jerked as if slapped. But Gloria spoke first: "Who's going to handle my career? You're on as my personal agent."

"You can have somebody else at the agency," Joe suggested. "There are a lot of bright young guys that—"

Harv Freeman shook his head. "I would rather have some easy to deal with guy—but I respect you, Joe...and I see no reason why things can't be smoothed out, You're quite right, this is not the time to argue things."

The doctor came out of Karla Kane's room, said: "You can go in Mr. Blake. She asked to talk to you, personally."

His words were directed to Joe.

"Be kind to her," his father suggested.

"Look, I'll handle this my way, okay?" He looked from one person to another, and nobody disagreed. Even Carol nodded, understandingly. She gave him a brave smile.

Stepping into the room, Joe moved to the bedside of the shockingly pale woman. For a moment it was difficult to realize this sickly looking creature was Karla Kane, the woman who had demanded so much from him in such a cruel manner.

She looked up at him, a weak smile on her face. Reaching out a hand, she waited for him to take hold of it.

"You don't...have to," she murmured in a weak voice.

He took the hand, squeezed it gently. Suddenly he felt more sorrow for Karla than anything else. She was, after all, a woman—a female, delicate and emotional. No matter how her personality had become twisted, she was somebody's little girl.

Before he could speak, Karla said weakly, "I've done a lot of foolish things, Joe...but ...this was probably the dumbest and smartest thing...almost too late I got to thinking about what you'd said...after you left...I started to make a call to some...friends, then stopped myself because suddenly I was crying and not knowing why...I went in to the bathroom...took a lot of sleeping pills and continued to think about what you'd said and...I guess you were right. The doctor said that my...physical condition is run down something terrible—that with the right food, a little rest and some shots...things will look...a lot better...and much different."

"Don't try to talk," Joe managed, a choke in his voice. For the first time he saw Karla for the total person she was. Regardless of everything, he could not help but feel emotional about it. Maybe in time they would become good friends.

She was saying: "I have to tell you...things. I feel rotten about how I treated you...and...I'm sorry I won't make any more demands...and I'll be a good girl...at the studio. You were right...I had to grow up...a little. Facing death made me realize that. I was terrified...Joe. Anything was better than death. Even getting old, living all by myself...anything. You...were right...there are a lot of guys I could like who...would like me. I had to prove something...guess I did...though not what I expected to..."

"Forget it. We can start over as friends—only. I'm afraid I'll be sorta tied up for life...but I want you to be my friend, Karla. Forget the past, and start over, new."

She nodded. "You're a good guy, Joe. What I did to you...I know you did only because...of responsibilities, and I guess for that little...innocent."

"What're you...?"

"Come on, admit it. You and Carol. If we're going to be friends, we best be honest. Want to be you're both in love?"

"I only bet on a sure thing."

She nodded, knowingly. "You're okay. Enjoy her. She's a nice lady. She deserves a good man!"

Joe managed to smile, then released her hand. "I better not stay any longer. Just do what the doctor tells you. Once you're well, back to the studio."

She nodded. "I have a picture to...complete. Tell Harv I'm sorry."

"I'll tell him."

With that Joe left, closing the door behind him. He looked at the four people waiting in the hallway.

"Well?" Harv Freeman demanded.

"She'll be fine. I don't think you'll ever have any trouble with her, Harv. Something happened to Karla. You'll see the moment you look at her. She's changed. Maybe...facing death."

His father nodded. "The doctor said she was badly run down...going through the change and well, that does do strange things to a woman. He claimed that it would be possible to make things easier. Also, said they'd have the staff headshrinker come in and have a chat with Karla before she leaves the hospital."

Harv shrugged. "I'll just have to shoot around her. The film is almost completed, anyway."

Carol took his hand, said: "We also had a little talk while you were in there. You'll stay at the agency, Joe—or both us girls leave it. We go with you. Your father will step down and put you in charge. Harv thinks you have the guts and know-how to handle anybody in Hollywood. So, your father will be taking a long vacation to Europe, shortly."

"Hey, not so fast!" Joe cried. "I'll...need some help and—"

Mr. Blake laughed. "There are a lot of good boys there, and my secretary can actually handle almost every legal problem to come up and...I won't leave for a couple of months. But...the agreement was that I don't put any more weird suggestions in your head, as this young girl stated in no uncertain terms." He nodded toward Carol. "Seems she has plans for you."

As the older men were chuckling, Joe announced: "To say nothing about the plans I have for her."

Without another word, he led Carol Fenton down the hall, leaving the others in a stunned quiet.

"How'd you manage all that?" Joe cried in surprise.

Carol squeezed his arm, said: "You'd be surprised how powerful a woman's words can be, under the right circumstances. And that Gloria is a doll—she likes you a lot and seems to think she owes you everything she has gotten.

160

When I started pressuring your father, she backed me to the hilt. Then, when Harv Freeman backed both of us—what could he do? Seems you have a talent with women—and studio bosses."

As they stepped out into the Hollywood night, a cool breeze whipping along the street, Carol requested: "Now, would you mind terribly going back to your apartment and continuing where you left off?"

"Yes, as a matter of fact, I would very much mind," Joe announced, ushering her to the car where it was parked a few yards away. "I'm going to make you an offer, and you either take it or leave it—totally."

"That sounds very ominous."

"It's really quite simple. I'll not have any woman I'm about to marry sleep with an unmarried man. So...you will say yes to the following."

"Yes?"

"You have enough clothing on to make a trip and don't need any more!"

"Yes...anything you say, dear."

"You like Las Vegas."

"Yes."

"You don't mind having a whole new closet of clothing—bought in the next couple of days."

"Yes." She laughed. "Rather, yes I'd like that!"

"You will enjoy a champagne flight across the stateline."

"Yes."

"And, naturally you will get married to Mr. Joe Blake immediately upon arriving in Las Vegas. I don't dare take a young woman across state lines for immoral purposes, you know. That could get me in big trouble!"

"Yes, darling." Then after a short silence, she asked: "Is that all?"

"All?"

"Yes!"

"That's all that's necessary."

"Then, now can we go to your apartment?"

"What in the hell for?"

"Well you might need a few things before taking such a

long trip and then we could go to my apartment, afterwards and—"

"We will right now go to the Los Angeles International Airport and get tickets for the first flight to Vegas and—"

She looked up into his eyes, gently kissed his lips. "Darling, please, you will do what I tell you?"

"To hell I will. I've had enough of women telling me what to do. In this family, I'll wear the pants. Do you agree?"

With a shrug, Carol embraced him. "Well, what the blazes are we waiting for? You did demand that I say yes to your requests! Vegas, here we come."

About the Author

Charles Nuetzel was born in San Francisco in 1934, and writes:

"As long as I can remember I wanted to be a writer. It was a dream I never thought would materialize. But with the help of Forrest J Ackerman, who became my agent, I managed to finally make it into print.

"I was lucky enough not only in selling my work to publishers but also ending up packaging books for some of them, and finally becoming a 'publisher' much like those who had bought my first novels. From there it as a simple leap to editing not only a sci-fi anthology, but a line of sci-fi books for Powell Sci-Fi back in the 1960s. Throughout these active professional years I had the chance to design some covers and do graphic cover layouts for pocket books & magazines."

Much of his work in covers and graphics are a result of having had a father who was a professional commercial artist, and who did a number of covers for sci-fi magazines in the 1950s and later for pocket books—even for some of Mr. Nuetzel's books.

In retirement he has become involved in swing dancing, a long time lover of Big Band jazz. But more interestingly world travels have taken him (and his wife Brigitte) across the world, to Hawaii, Caribbean, Mexico, Kenya, Egypt, Peru, having a lifelong interest in ancient civilizations. His website is full of thousands of pictures taken during these trips.